MALICIOUS

MALICIOUS

REMONA G. TANNER

authorHOUSE®

AuthorHouse™
1663 Liberty Drive
Bloomington, IN 47403
www.authorhouse.com
Phone: 1 (800) 839-8640

Published by AuthorHouse 04/17/2017

ISBN: 978-1-5246-8812-7 (sc)
ISBN: 978-1-5246-8811-0 (e)

Library of Congress Control Number: 2017905783

Print information available on the last page.

This book is printed on acid-free paper.

It's frightening, releasing your interpretation of art into the world. Our world is such a scary, hypercritical place. I've seen it eat people alive, devastating criticism crushing their very desire to create. Then they become unable to create, stalled and afraid to be artists, so they settle for being normal. Some people measure their success by how many feathers they can ruffle, the way some politicians do. Others measure their success by how many heads they can get to nod in acceptance. Either way, negative feedback can break your spirit. We're all sensitive about our work whether we admit it or not. So I guess putting your work out there is the true definition of courage. As if to say, *Go ahead; make or break me.*

"Pain is a birthright too, even more so than happiness." I once heard that, and it stayed with me. Thank you, Momma and Larissa. The Bible promised our days would be filled with troubles. It would do no justice to keep the overcoming of these troubles to ourselves; they plant knowledge so that wisdom can take root and blossom. Every stumble is not only forgiven but acknowledged and rebuked and considered progression. Maybe that's how we should look at one another's path, with patience, tolerance, and understanding. Maybe then the world would be a better place. I hope I live long enough to see that world come to life.

Hannah, you've set the bar higher than any of us could have ever imagined. For the rest of your life, you will be living and breathing proof that God does not make mistakes.

Nikki, I know you think you never cross our minds, but we miss you every single day. You haven't been forgotten and you never will. You stay with us in our hearts, and you'll be there forever. This is for you …

Prologue

Breathe … breathe … breathe …

She paced. Halo could barely identify the echo of her own thoughts over the deafening high-pitched ringing in her ear. The sound of the gunshots seemed to pierce her temples and stagger the thoughts attempting to register in her mind, making it difficult to comprehend what was happening. *Why can't I get up? Why can't I move?*

Halo, growing weaker by the second from the yawning wound tunneled deep in her chest, managed to lift her limp right arm and clutch her left shoulder. Beneath her cold coarse palm, leaking from what felt like a stinging heap of hot jumping nerves, was warm, wet saturation. It was blood, obviously. *There's a hole straight through my body. I've been shot. In fact … I think I'm dying.*

Breathe … breathe … breathe … don't freak out, Halo thought, encouraging herself to ease the progressively growing panic. She stared at the weather-stained ceiling tiles.

The room seemed to have an active heartbeat and a swift pulse of its own living deep in the walls, making them move in and out like a giant pair of lungs, a hallucination generated by excessive blood loss, no doubt. *Get up. Move now.*

Spine-chilling screams resonated from the back where the dressing room was. Multiple shots quickly followed, ceasing the terrified cries. Halo was suddenly aware of the horror that would later be one of the most scandalous massacres of all time. To Halo's left, coughing massive clots of blood and saliva, lay Whisper, her petite ribcage faintly heaving.

Halo managed to roll over onto her belly and slowly crawl, maneuvering beside Whisper. "It's me. It's Halo. You're not alone. I'm here."

Whisper's eyes widened at the sound of a familiar voice, and her body convulsed as she struggled to hold on and speak.

"You have to be quiet," Halo muttered, fearing they'd be overheard. "We gotta get outta here. I need you to roll onto your stomach and crawl with me as best you can. I see the door from here. It's not that far; we can make it, but we must move right now! You've got to get strong *fast* if we're going to make it out of here alive. Can you do that for me? Whisper … Whisper?"

With one final trembling exhale, Whisper was dead.

Before Halo could cry, she heard glass crunching beneath the assailant's feet. The sound grew nearer. "Would it make you happy to hear me beg? Would that please you? If I begged, 'Don't kill me. Please spare me'?" Halo asked, delirium growing.

Halo looked up. "You think you're special? You ain't nothing but another tragedy under this club's belt, a weakling from the very beginning! Another lost soul in the trophy case to be counted and ruminated over. My hurt doesn't give me the right to murder. What makes your pain more privileged than mine? Will death make everything okay again? Taking all these innocent lives?" She coughed into her arm, the pain making her grimace.

"No," she continued. "You'll still be damaged goods inside. In fact, you'll be in worse shape than ever before because you will have traded your soul for a little bit of revenge. Yeah, you let the devil rip you off. You made a bad deal. Murders ain't fit for heaven, and you know it. How do you feel now? Bet it still hurts." Halo laughed feverishly, eyelids heavier now.

"Well, I won't beg. So … don't count on it. Never begged anyone for anything in my whole life. There's a difference between being proud of what you do and not being ashamed of what you do. Proud? No! Never were we so dumb. Ashamed? No! Never were we ever so naïve; to think that things in life are free, so how could we be? I'll die knowing that I did my best for my daughter here on earth, and when the dust finally settles she'll remember her mother's strength and not her bad decisions, though there were many. Who keeps count? So kill me! I'll go up first and save the nearest cloud for my child right beside me. I would say, 'See you later,' but you won't be welcome there now for all this blood you spilled. Send me to heaven—go ahead! I'm waiting! Even beasts like me are welcome there! Do it if you have any valor left at all!"

Eight hours prior …

"When was your last confession, my child?"

"It's been so long; I honestly find it difficult to remember."

"That's all right. The last time is not as crucial to your salvation as the reason you're here today. You have already been forgiven for your transgressions. Shall we focus on what troubles you now?"

"It's shame, Father. I am utterly ashamed. I've become an ornament to be ogled, not adored or honored the unsoiled way God intended when he created me in my mother's womb. I've fallen hard, corrupted on my broken crown and molted wings. I'm ill with the filthy, staring eyes of this world. The eyes, they were all over me and I felt them. It felt like an itch, a grating discomfort that made me squirm because I knew all along it was wrong. I've never felt dirtier. It's an impurity that cannot be washed, only burned and purged."

"Confess, my child. I cannot fathom the weight of your burdens. Unload them now. His heart is ready to receive your sin, and forgiveness is yours to claim if you chose to turn away from your wicked ways and never return to them."

"I thank you for the opened door. But I cannot turn away just yet. They will pay the debt of my tears. I will collect. I did not come here for forgiveness. I came to pray for them, that they are not turned away from the pearly gates on sight. You see, I'm sending them all up long before their time."

"Vengeance is not ours to seek, my child. Revenge is an honor and curse that we must never take upon ourselves. You know this."

"But I must! My virtue is all gone, spent. And there is a price tag on their heads for it."

What about my heart?
What about my soul?
So little left of thyself,
To banish, to kill
To mount upon your shelf.

Fear never had so many faces ...
In the form of distrust,
Draped in disloyalty,
Illustrated in a portrait of a crooked smile
In weary blistered feet, worn from miles.

Diamonds in the sky? Us? Not likely
Rainbows in the clouds? We? No such luck
More like rocks in the dirt
Conscious mind far too relaxed now
Slept on every warning, no intruder alert.

You see our worth had been ...
Measured and weighed.
Calculated down to the very last flaw
And we were forced to be
Whatever *they* decided, whatever *they* saw.

Pill-induced depressions,
Forgotten dreams by the dozen
Afraid to move forward
No taking it back, no reverse
No longer growing, suddenly frozen.

Enter hell ... once upon a dream,
Twice upon a nightmare
Come on in and sit for a spell.
Pull up a chair, spark a conversation
With the devil, if you dare ...

Que sera, whatever will be,
And it's not what it ain't ...
We got scars, we got sins, no angels, no saints.
Not exactly freedom, not exactly chained.
It's malicious, not pretty. It's not liberty or fame.

Chapter 1

"Tommy! Where are my note cards? I've told you a million times: don't move my things! Tommy! Get in here! Note cards! I can't find them!"

The makeup technician struggled to apply bronzer to Diana's face as her arms flailed every which way. "Tommy!" she continued, ranting until he finally burst through the trailer door, knocking a few daytime television awards from the shelf.

"Note cards? I've got them right here, Ms. Foxx. Don't fret," Tommy said, his voice annoyingly high-pitched due to the ear bud blasting concert techno in one ear.

"What took you so long? Once, just once, could I get an intern who performs as if he desires long-term employment?" a frustrated Diana complained. "I need your performance level tripled today. Can't you see how scattered I am? I'm more nervous than when I covered that sleazy-mayor-mistress scandal last fall."

"Take a chill pill, Ms. Foxx. You'll appear polished and prepared and professional, as always," Tommy said. "It's not like you're interviewing the president."

"You're right! It's not like that at all. It's far more exciting than a presidential affair. Today, *I* make history. I've been given the opportunity of a lifetime to pick the brain of a real survivor. She is such a rare exception. This interview will change the course of my career. I just know it. Yes, from here on out, the direction is up. I've been waiting on a chance like this for a long time. I won't stand for any careless mistakes!"

"Yeah, I guess she is kind of a big deal locally," Tommy said.

"Locally? Do you ever take a break from your virtual reality games and unsuccessful social media flirting? She's so much more than a familiar face strutting around this town." Tommy's head tilted back involuntarily, rolling his eyes. As if he hadn't already heard the facts a thousand times before. "National news executives flew in from all over the country, stampeding the hospital to hound her. They camped on her lawn for days, begging for the scoop, but she refused to talk. *Until now.* For reasons I'll never understand, she's decided to give *us* the exclusive—a station whose high point this year was the county fair's pumpkin pie-eating contest. Everyone's going to be watching tonight's segment. I'm sweating like a pig at a luau. I've got steel butterflies fluttering in my stomach. I've chewed my nails down to the cuticle, and I keep getting nervous hiccups."

"Do you think she'll sign my Club Malice T-shirt?"

A look of utter disgust slowly settled on Diana's face, and she sighed heavily, as if near wit's end. "Sign ... your ... T-shirt? Could you be more insensitive? Do you even know who she is? She's the sole survivor of the Club Malice massacre. Eleven people are dead—heinously murdered in cold blood. I highly doubt she's interested in autographing your cheap memorabilia trash."

"But I got the matching hat. There was a kiosk outside the hospital. They sold like hotcakes."

"You're an exhausting example of incompetence and sheer ignorance. That is what I'm tempted to write on your performance review every time I see your face. If stupidity were contagious, you'd be patient zero and we'd all be quarantined for being within a mile of you, dummy. Get out of my sight! Come and get me the minute she steps foot on set," Diana commanded.

"Oh, I forgot. She's already here," a dumbfounded Tommy said.

"What?" Diana yelled, smacking the makeup artist's brush from her face.

"She's already here. She arrived about twenty minutes ago. She's with the audio squad being prepped with her lapel mic. I'm sorry. I meant to tell you."

Diana sprang into action, shoving him from her path. "You imbecile! Why didn't you say so up front? I can't keep her waiting! What's wrong with you? I have half a mind to make a few calls, double-check those high school electives you claim to have under your belt! The way you perform, it's hard to believe you even have a diploma!"

"Sorry, boss. I got a little distracted trying to work the cappuccino machine. There are so many buttons. Anyhow, she's waiting in the green room. But before you head in, Mr. Pete wants to see you in his office."

"Fine. Get to the green room and see if she needs any refreshments. If she wants something we don't have, jump on your bike and go buy it with your own money. If you try to get her to sign anything, you'll be mopping floors at night to pay your rent. I'll destroy your career hopes so severely that you'll need to start all over in community college just to stay out of a cardboard box on the street."

The hallway parted like the Red Sea as a determined Diana rushed through. Workers in lower departments looked down and scurried to the nearest corners to keep from becoming victims of her wrath.

While feared for her aggressive approach to productivity, Diana's reputation for professionalism had paved the way for her budding career. She had a knack for getting things done the right way by demanding respect and precision. In a short three years, she'd managed to turn an entry level errand position into an esteemed anchor position. That had set the pace for her life: get to the top by any means necessary. People expected a certain level of quality from her, and although it earned her respect, it secretly frightened her.

It was twenty-five years since Pete Pierson took over the station. At times he found his own success hard to believe. How did a meek freelance journalist became a network tycoon? It was a mystery to many, but Pete had been his father's successor, the greatest commentator the network had ever seen. *If only he'd lived longer. He would have been proud,* Pete thought as he sat in his office contemplating his achievements.

"You wanted to see me, Mr. Pete?" Diana asked, tapping on the door while poking her head inside.

"Diana, so good to see you. Yes, come on in. Take a seat."

Diana sat, eyeing her watch.

"Relax. You've got time to sit and chat before the interview starts," he said, grinning, exposing a chunk of mutilated lunch still lodged between his two front teeth. "You excited?"

"Yes, sir, I am. I'd like to thank you again for giving me this break to prove that I'm more than capable of running your station upon your retirement."

"Don't go treating this interview like an audition to inherit my position. It wounds my pride. It makes me think you can't wait to see me go. It makes me feel territorial. And don't thank me. Allowing you to air the interview on my station, yes, I gave the green light on that, but she asked for you by name. Said she only wanted to talk to you or no deal. Imagine my surprise, getting that call. Hell, I got two other anchors with seniority, real pit bulls who get out there and expose the facts. You've been here for such a short time and she picks you. Odd, isn't it?"

"Consider it odd if you wish. Maybe it's pure luck."

"I don't believe in luck, Ms. Foxx. Whatever the reason, this is your golden ticket straight to the top. Don't mess this up."

"Is that all, sir?"

"Yes. Good luck."

Diana entered the green room, prompting more haste and bustle from the television crew working inside. She managed four footsteps before being ambushed by audio support.

The set coordinator followed close. "We're all set to shoot. We've set the room at a comfortable sixty-seven degrees, with dim lighting for the softening effect you requested. You'll find warm tea with lemon on the right side of your chair out of camera view so that your voice is smooth and clear, the way you like it."

Diana managed a slight nod every few seconds to appear attentive but was secretly tuning them out. She was scanning the room for Reese.

Diana focused on a pile of uniformed techs flocking the chair opposite the one reserved for her. The workers disbursed like a flock of spooked crows at Diana's approach.

The sight of Reese caused Diana to pause. Reese's face was innocent, so adolescent, and she appeared nervous—almost afraid, like a tiny mouse. Diana found it difficult to believe such a sweet, gentle girl could be caught up in such a disturbing ordeal.

No, the face didn't match the story one bit.

"Ms. Reese Tania, as I live and breathe. At the risk of sounding like a bloodthirsty fan, I must say it's an honor to finally meet you face-to-face," Diana said, extending a shaky, sweaty palm.

"Fan? No, I could never consider you a vampire like all the rest. The honor is all mine. Believe me. I've always admired your ambition. I've followed your work for a long time. You came out to our university campus a few years back for career day. Your speech was unbelievably humble—all the parts about not forgetting where you come from. I was too shy to meet you back then, plus the long line of frat guys gawking at you made it difficult to get anywhere near you. My day doesn't start until I watch your segment on *Wake up, East Mossvilla.*"

Her gentle voice made Diana smile genuinely—kind of how an adult would smile at a little child expressing admiration to her hero. "Really? Thank you. I don't know what to say. Hearing you speak so highly of me, I'm filled with gratitude. But I'm not the superstar here. To be honest, I'm quite nervous. You're the highest-profile assignment I've ever taken on. I have so many questions for you, Reese. One of them is the reason you're here. Not that I'm not happy you picked us. I'm just curious. Why us? Why this network? Why me?"

Kirk, the main cameraman, zoomed in and focused on Reese's sudden sheltered demeanor.

"Back off!" Diana yelled. "Have you no professional finesse? Show some self-control, for goodness sake! This interview has not started yet! Stand down!" She turned her attention back to Reese. "Vultures. I'm sorry about that."

"It's okay, really. I expected everyone to be a bit *anxious*, to say the least. I'm looking forward to it, finally talking about it. I pray that I'll feel lighter in my spirit once it's all revealed—the truth and the tragedy that is now my namesake."

"*Lighter in your spirit?* What a beautiful way to describe what we're going to accomplish here on today." Diana sat back in her chair, crossing her long, elegant legs. She eyed her watch again—four minutes until showtime. "Can I get someone to pour you a cup of coffee? A cool bottle of fruit-infused water? A snack? Anything to make you more comfortable?"

"No. I'm as comfortable as possible for now. But there is one thing."

"Yes. Yes, to whatever you need," Diana answered eagerly.

"This happening—it's my story. It's our story. Like you said before, you have questions, everyone does, and I promise we'll get to all of them in due time, but I would like to start from the very beginning. You want me—well, the mirrors in my soul take no prisoners and pay no homage. There is only the truth. The beginning—only then will you be able to truly understand it all."

The lighting crew eyed the camera crew, and they all swapped curious glances at Diana as if they all felt the same grave chill from the severity of Reese's glare.

Diana looked down at her carefully worded, premeditated inquiries she'd taken the time out to write and then back up at Reese. "Of course, … the beginning." Diana hesitated, cueing the camera man for countdown, turning left for a close up.

And in five … four … three … two …

"Good evening, East Mossvilla. I'm Diana Foxx, bringing the hottest controversial topics right into your living room. I'm here today with *the* Reese Tania. Get comfy at home, and join us as we dive deep into the most terrifying mass murder ever to curse America's backyard. I've been asked to advise viewer discretion."

Diana turned back to Reese. "Thank you for joining us today."

"Thank you for having me," Reese said, looking directly into the camera and then up at the lights.

"Start whenever you're ready," Diana whispered.

Reese nodded and cleared her throat. "Who's the bad guy? Who's the infamous bad guy? Every story has one, a villain. And if there's no bad guy in their version of the story, someone's lying or hiding something. Who's the menace? I know you wanna know. The problem is, no one wants to own up to the chaos. In fact, people would rather point a hundred fingers accusing a hundred different people than take claim for what they contributed to the bedlam. Cowards."

Reese appeared nauseous with anxiety but determined. She continued after a deep breath. "I wanna be clear about one thing. Before I unravel this story for you, there's something I need you to understand. It's always the customers—they're the bad guys. Not the managers, not the club owners, not the dancers or the bartenders or the DJs. Only the customers. Without the demand for depravity in this world, there'd be no supply.

"By demand for depravity I mean the carnal, animalistic perversion of the body and mind. By supply I mean those of us who recognize the snakes in the world but do not run from them, instead making them bend to our will. Yes, we charmed them like cobras rising from dirty wicker baskets, enthralled by the sound of our voice. I'm going to tell you everything; the good, the bad, the ugly, and the ungodly. So I hope your ears aren't modest or this is going to be a long, rough hour for you. I won't adjust the truth or manipulate it for you, so don't ask me to. I won't embellish or diminish it at all. I'll say it once more, only the *customers* are the bad people. Not us. If you plan on branding us malicious human beings, tell me now. I can get up and leave before we waste time. It's not us, we're not bad. Do you understand that?"

"Yes," Diana said.

"Good."

Chapter 2

"Why do you think people are drawn to the darkness?"

"Well, I'm not sure," Diana answered, looking around first, as if the question had been addressed to someone else.

"I'll tell you why. The devil has tricked them into seeing no future for themselves in the light. The darkness … it just makes more sense when you're lost and tired of wandering aimlessly with no purpose, just wishing and hoping one day you'll be good enough for certain people and certain places. It's … knowing you're different in a bad way; like maybe you've seen too much to be pure or done too many misdeeds to deserve peace. If you feel like the light doesn't want you, you completely turn the other way instead of being an orphan. You find a place to … belong.

"Everything has a dawn and a dusk. True to the sun's nature, the beginning was bright, dare I say promising. Toward the end of it all, the darkness consumed and all the goodness weakened like the dusk's devouring. I heard the thunder long before I saw the lightning, but it was too late by then, too late to run and hide, too late to take shelter. All that was left to do was brace yourself, hope for the best. It was the twenty-third year of my life. It was the longest year I'd ever lived—365 days just the same as all the others but far longer in terms of growth. I learned so much about the universe and its bizarre people. I think back to when I was just a little girl. At night, I'd lay in bed and scream for my mother because I was too afraid to swing my feet over the side of my bed. I feared a monster would grab my ankles and pull me under. And if I was lucky enough to outrun that monster, then surely the one hiding in the closet behind the hangers would get me. Back then those were my worst fears. Simple, irrational, but easy to understand if you consider the mentality of a child. But that was a very long time ago. When you grow up, you get scared of other things, and those things are far more difficult to make sense of but twice as hard to overcome.

"Have you ever been played with gasoline? I have. I remember the smell of it. The fluid was all over my clothes, and it burned my eyes as I wiped my tears while driving down the old dirt road right outta city limits. It was a detour I hadn't intended to take but the rain beating down on my windshield made it difficult to pay attention to things like red lights and street signs. My fury had caused a migraine to settle in as a throbbing, stubborn lump right in the center of my forehead. I wasn't paying attention to where I was going at all.

"In the midst of all the bedlam, my car swerved in and out of my lane, and my mother's voice came to mind: 'Never drive upset. Never. That's how we lost your sister, and I won't lose you the same way.' There weren't many cars on the road, but the few that passed were honking and flashing their headlights.

"'I won't lose two daughters on the asphalt.' There it was again, her voice, chiming in the back of my mind. I decided to pull over. There was an empty parking lot off the side of the road so I swung in. I killed the engine and buried my face in my hands and sobbed. I don't know how long I sat there, but I didn't move until the sound of the big purple light at the top of the tall pole switching on startled me. It was a loud buzzing noise, somewhat similar to the sound of bugs frying in a camp lantern. It flickered, illuminating a giant neon woman who blew kisses. She entranced me, blinking on and off.

"There was a man in a yellow raincoat standing beneath it, smoking a cigarette. We made eye contact for a second and he began to walk over. I struggled with my keys, trying to crank the car and speed off before he got close, but before I could separate the car key from all the other keys on my keychain, he was tapping at my window. Mistaking him for a homicidal drifter, I cracked the window just enough to inhale his second-hand smoke, no more no less.

"'You know you're on private property, right?' he asked in somewhat of a joking manner.

"No. I'm sorry. I didn't know. I was just leaving anyway.

"'Looks like you've been doing some crying.'

"No," I lied.

"'You sure 'bout that? I ain't no genius, but your eyes look a little misty to me.'

"Yes, I'm crying. I mean I was … but that's none of your business. I honestly didn't mean to trespass. I was just looking for a place to collect myself. I'll go.

"'Well, hold on now. Forgive my lack of manners,' he said, his voice softer. 'Didn't anybody ever tell you It's bad luck to drive when you're all emotional? That's the best way to get yourself involved in a car accident.'

"Actually, yes. My mother did.

"'Well, she's a wise woman. Why don't you come on in and have a drink on me?'

"I really shouldn't. I'm not much of a drinker, and I don't talk to strangers.

"'Okay. My name's Jack. Jack of all trades, that's what they call me around here. What's your name?'

"Reese.

"'It's nice to meet you, Reese. See now, we ain't strangers no more. So what do you say? Have a drink with a new friend? Wait out this rain?'

"The gravel underneath my flip flops sounded like a demon chewing rock candy. The worn steel wailed as the door opened and screamed even louder when it slammed shut behind me.

"I sat at the bar with Jack standing directly across, a dirty washcloth thrown over one shoulder. 'Are you a bartender?' I asked.

"'Yes, all trades. That means I master many things. I run this place, and I just happen to mix a hell of a drink. So, pick your poison. What do you like, clear or brown? I can mix both if you don't mind a light hangover.'

"'I guess one drink is just as good as the next. Anything to make me numb, specifically my heart.'

"'Something numbing for the heart. I got just the thing.'

"'What's this?' I asked, letting its bitter sweetness soak into my taste buds.

"'That there is a Washington apple. I don't wanna brag, but I hear I make the best one in town. What do you think?'

"'It's really good, but I guess I'd have to taste all the others in town to be a fair judge.'

"He laughed. 'Honest. Funny. I like you.'

"'I'm okay I guess,' I muttered, sipping.

"'So, what's the plan? How long you gonna cry? How long you gonna let yourself to be so sad? You gonna let some loser keep you in this bad a condition?'

"'You think a guy caused me to be like this?'

"'I'm wiser than I look, and I done seen that look on a girl's face once or twice. Hell, I've caused that look on many women's faces in the past. Answer the question. How long?'

"'I don't know.'

"'What do you mean?'

"'Right now, I just feel so ... so ...'

"'Broken? Defeated?'

"'Yes, both.'

"'No!' Jack yelled, slamming his fist on the bar top. 'Those are the things we *never* allow ourselves to feel.'

"'But that's what I'm feeling.'

"'Self-esteem all depreciated, Right? Tell me, do you feel weak?'

"'Yes," I said slowly, waiting for him to smack the bar again, but he didn't.

"'I don't think you're weak at all.'

"'You don't even know me.'

"'You're a woman. That's enough to prove me right.'

"'So simply being a woman makes me strong?'

"'No, being a woman aware of her capabilities, worth, and power makes you strong.'

"'Me, strong?'

"'Very much so ...'

"'I don't feel very strong. I feel like I've been robbed of something.'

"'I know a way you can get some of yourself back if you want.'

"'Really? How?' I finished my drink with one gulp.

"'Turn around.'

"That's when I first saw it. The stage and all the empty chairs and ash trays. The answer was obvious but I asked anyway. 'Is that a stripper pole?'

"'Well it sure as hell ain't no telephone pole. It ain't the north pole either. Do I look like Santa to you?' he responded with a smirk, throwing back a vodka shot. 'I've seen a lot of women pass through here. Most of them down and out, but I never call them lost causes. The ones looking for short-term definition, they stroll in here with generic identities and fade into the background once they're done acting out. Who knows why, maybe their daddies didn't teach them how to love or their mommas never told them about God. Some come to release their inner bad girl for the first time in their boring lives. No matter the reason, they *all* leave stronger and thousands of dollars richer.'

"'Thousands?'

"'Cold hard cash, no checks or pay periods. I wouldn't lie to you, couldn't if I wanted to, you look like you got a good head on your shoulders. You'd probably see right through me if I tried. I think you're smart enough to use this business in a way that it will *never* be able to use and abuse you.'

"'I don't know. I've never danced a day in my life, especially not half-dressed in a room full of people I never met. I go to Bible study.'

"'Well, here's my card. You know where to find me. If you're brave enough to come back, I'll take you under my wing. No harm will ever come to you. I don't make promises I can't keep. And if it makes you feel better, you can even bring your Bible with you.'

"'I think the rain's all done. Thanks for the drink and the talk. It was nice of you.'

"'Anytime. Now you go on home and think about it. And if you decide you really 'bout that life, come on back, Mafia.'

"'Mafia?' And what did ''bout that life' even mean?

"'Yeah. That's what I'm gonna call you from now on. One day I'd love to hear about why you walked in here smelling like an arsonist.'

"Walking back to my car, I looked up at the neon sign, twirling the card between my knuckles. *'Bout that life* … I still don't know what it means.

Chapter 3

"I don't know what made me go back. Staring in the mirror half-naked my first night employed as an entertainer at Club Malice, I second-guessed my decision. In fact, I questioned it three or four times. *What am I doing here?* I asked myself, looking around as if people could hear my thoughts.

"I couldn't stop throwing up, no matter how hard I tried.

"'You gonna leave any food in your stomach, or you gonna puke it all in my trashcan?' Jack joked, handing me a can of soda.

"'I'm trying. I'm just so ...'

"'Nervous?'

"'Hell yeah,' I answered, wiping my face with the back of my hand.

"'Don't be. Hardest part is getting 'em to double take and you look good, so half the work is already done. Trust me, if you looked bad I'd tell you and still be able to sleep at night. You'll do just fine. I've seen less potential prosper in here.'

"'But I've never danced on a pole before. I'm going to make a fool of myself.'

"'Okay, so you never danced. But you're pretty. I can work with pretty. You can be taught to dance well, what's not a talent is a skill. Thank God skills can be taught or else I wouldn't have a business. Ugly ... I can't work with ugly. Who wants attention from a sea hag? Nobody, that's who. I got a girl coming in early to show you how things work around here. Put a cold rag on your face and get out there on the floor. She'll be here soon. Too late to turn back now,' he said with a smirk.

"'Am I safe? With all the men in here?'

"'I told you, no harm will come to you.'

"'Do you promise?'

"'Here—I've got something for you.' Jack reached into his back pocket. 'This is my favorite pocket knife. I won it in a poker game, cheated it out of some old gambler who bragged too much. Now I don't allow anybody but security to carry any weapons in my club, but I'll make an exception for you. I want you to hold onto it until you feel safe, whether that's a day or a year. Then you can give it back.'

"I slowly reached for it. 'Are you sure it's okay?'

"'Go on, tuck it away before the others see. I don't need nobody complaining about special treatment; that's how rumors start. I wouldn't trust half these girls with a sharpened pencil.'

"After there was literally no more food left in me, I made my way to the bar. I sat alone, trying not to draw any attention.

"After a while a plump gentleman pulled up a stool beside me. 'It'd be an honor to buy you a drink, beautiful lady; would that be all right with you?' he asked innocently. He was handsome for an older gentleman. I blushed a tad. It seemed like a harmless gesture, so I obliged.

"'Yes, sure. That'd be nice.' He proceeded to order a drink from the opposite end of the bar and walked it back to me.

"'Thank you. What's your name?' I asked, trying to casually spark conversation. Just as I lifted the glass to my lips, a strange woman approached, crudely snatching if from my grasp.

"'She's not thirsty, Percy!' she snapped, eyes intensely locked on him. 'Do yourself a favor and slink to another barstool before I go get Harris on you. You've been warned about this before.'

"Without saying a word, he slid away, chastised eyes facing the floor.

"She sat in his place and scanned me from head to toe. 'You must be the new girl Jack told me about.'

"'Yeah.'

"'What are they calling you?'

"'Mafia.'

"'Mafia?'

"'Yeah, Jack picked it. It's kind of a long story.'

'"Well, if Jack picked it, you must have earned it somehow. A long story, you say? If you keep taking drinks from barflies you don't know, like Percy the pervert, you won't live long to tell it.'

'"Did I do something wrong?'

'"Wrong? No. You got a customer to buy you a drink. Congratulations, you earned the club ten dollars. You didn't do anything wrong, but you did do something deadly,' she declared, holding the glass near my face so that I could see a tiny white tablet slowly dissolving behind the cherry tint of the alcoholic beverage.

'"Oh God …' I muttered, thankful to nearly tears.

'"Yeah, *Oh God* is right. Don't ever let a customer handle your drink, that's the number one rule. You either take it from the bartender's hand yourself or you let it sit on the table until the ice turns it to water. You're new here, fresh meat. They can smell your inexperience; it's like a pheromone. Everybody's gunning for you, so stay on high alert. Everyone here is the devil until they show you a pair of angel wings, you hear me? Everyone's the devil, men and women. I'll show you who you should steer clear of, people like Percy the pervert.'

'"Percy the pervert? That's his name?'

'"Yeah, he earned his alias just like we earned ours. He's in here the minute we open and don't leave until he's done hunting. His usual prey—dumb new girls.'

'"Hunting?'

'"You're not ready for that talk yet. Jack will have my head if I run you off on your first night. I'm Valentine, by the way. Valentine, like the holiday. It's nice to meet you.'

'"What's your real name?'

'"That's rule number two. Don't go asking people their real name, and don't go telling people yours. If they wanna tell you who they are, they'll do so on their own terms; don't go snooping and prying. That's the best say to make enemies in here, forgetting to mind your own business. You will call me Valentine. I don't like my real name anyhow. I was named by my father. I hate my father.'

'"Well, it's nice to meet you too, Valentine.'

'"You smoke? Cigarettes or weed?'

'"Neither.'

"'That's cool. I smoke both. Most of us do, just don't get caught if you pick up the habit. Sometimes we all hang out back by the tracks. You can come with; you'll probably learn more out there chewing the fat than you will in here. I'll wait to smoke; first I'll take you to meet some of the evil shrews you'll be hustling with.'

"'This is important: get familiar with security. Know where your security guard is standing at all times. You're going to need them every single night.'

"Valentine tapped a tall giant on the shoulder. He slowly turned around, and I had to tilt my head back to clearly see his face.

"'Harris, meet Mafia. Mafia, this is Harris. If you have any problems with customers, you come and get him. He's a hell of a watchdog, mean like one too. He watches the camera close. If you're ever in trouble, turn to the camera and hold up three fingers. That's the distress signal here. He sees that, he's coming back to see about you right away.'

"'Nice to meet you,' I said, with a parched, nervous swallow.

"'Welcome,' he replied with a smile.

"'Come on, don't drag your feet. I got money coming in here tonight. I still gotta put my face on," Valentine said quickly as we ducked behind a beaded curtain. 'This is the DJ booth. Up here you can see the club from wall to wall. If you ever get lost or afraid, just come here and stay until I come get you. Saddle's a good DJ. He'll keep an eye on you.'

"'Hello, I'm Mafia.'

"'Saddle's the name, sweetheart. I'm know for giving the ladies the ride of their life,' he said with a sly Casanova wink.

"'Pay him no mind, he's just an old tease,' Valentine said, giving him a hug. 'Time to meet the girls. Hope you have a high tolerance for bull crap.'"

Chapter 4

"We couldn't have been more different. How dare critics put us in a box, limit our individuality? It's unfair how people decide who you are before you're given a proper chance to change their mind. But that's what we call unwarranted judgment. Judgment is not a victimless crime—it takes and takes until you become the very monster they deem you. That's a stranger's right, I guess, the right to call it like they see it, but what happens when there's more than what meets the eye? Drawn conclusions, at a glance—how inhumane. What if people cared enough to look just a little deeper, beyond the surface? Then you'd see just as many differences as similarities.

"'Seen one, seen 'em all.' 'Heard one sob story, heard 'em all.' People are ignorant, the majority anyway. I don't say that to be mean. It's just a cold, hard fact. They lack basic knowledge. That and many other important things like respect. Every snowflake that falls from the sky has been cut differently than all the others that fell from the very same sky. Dancers are like snowflakes, and we're still people. We all had goals, paths, and purposes. God gave us different roles to play and distinct ways to impact one another.

"When I recollect the night I met them all, I can't help but smile. You see, I was afraid they'd think I didn't belong there. If only I'd known how we all shared that same fear.

"Chatter ceased and heads turned as I walked in behind Valentine. The brief silence made me want to turn and run away, but thank God for Valentine. She always did know how to work a room; I'll give her that.

"'Hey, y'all, this Is Mafia. Jack told me to bring her on back and introduce her, so play nice.'

"Whisper was the first to welcome me. She had the most beautifully biblical hair I'd ever seen. It reminded me of golden threads, the kind that gave Samson his strength, like the Old Testament stated. It was the first thing I noticed about her. It smelled like apple cinnamon, and I admit some nights I hugged her just to inhale it for comfort. Whisper had a way of looking after us all, making sure to cook enough at home to bring leftovers for the girls who'd drink so much they'd forget to eat. She made sure the dressing room stayed stocked with hand sanitizer and deodorant and wrote daily quotes about the value of hard work on the mirrors in lipstick to keep us motivated.

"'The new girl! Hello! I'm Whisper. I would say we're happy to have you, but ending up here isn't necessarily a good thing, is it? So instead I'll say welcome to hell.'

"'Thank you, I appreciate it,' I replied, my hand out.

"'What's that?' Whisper asked, looking down at my hand as if she'd been terribly offended by it. 'I don't shake hands, I hug,' she said.

"It was as if Whisper knew I'd be around and that we'd eventually love one another like sisters. 'I've been here since the day this club opened. Yeah, I was the first girl on that stage out there. Those scuffmarks on the stage floor, they came from my heels. Been offered management status a few times. I could run this club with my eyes closed, but no thank you. I hate dancing. I hate the lifestyle. It's about the money for me. I've been saving my pennies. One day I'm going to use that money and open my own business. Then I'm gonna quit while there's still some youth left in my thighs.'

"'What kind of business?' I asked, filled with curiosity.

"'A place where women can learn how to pole dance, help them become comfortable in their skin again after they have babies and get all depressed about life. There's more to the pole than dollar bills. I'd like to open a place that promotes fitness and sexuality through exotic dance. A place where all women can channel their inner vixen.'

"'Would you just shut up? For the hundredth time, that is the stupidest idea I've ever heard!' The rude declaration flew out of nowhere like a heat-seeking fireball from the opposite end of the dressing room. Her name was January, like the first month of the year. She sat at the mirror, caking makeup on both cheeks. 'Why would you want to teach frumpy housewives to do what we do? If men have a show to watch at home, why would they need to come watch us? They come here to spend money. Don't be an idiot—your dream business is bad for *our* business. Any fool can see that.'

"Valentine leaned in near my ear. 'Don't pay her any mind. She's an emotional, inconsiderate wreck these days, stressing about her vile pit of a womb. Major fertility issues. She had a fourth miscarriage this year alone.'

"Whisper nudged Valentine. 'Hush. She doesn't really mean it. She's just hypersensitive today.'

"'My point is she's being a complete bitch, taking her frustration out on us. It's no one's fault but her own, her body being a toxic pit of vodka and all. Not our fault her uterus is defective.'

"'Defective uterus, maybe. But my hearing is just fine, Valentine!' barked a cranky January.

"'Good!' Valentine said, walking me around to meet everyone else.

"I met Halo with the perfect brown-sugar skin, cherry dyed hair, and flawless makeup. She made it painfully clear there was no room in her heart for a boyfriend or a best friend; God and her daughter had filled it up. There was Olive with the big green lotus tattoo covering her entire back from shoulder blade to shoulder blade, and long bangs that shadowed her mysterious eyes.

"There was Sage, who was undeniably forever young. A little older than the rest of us but still just as beautiful. She had been bartending since she was a teen and not ashamed to admit she was looking for love, which in my opinion made her courageous. 'One day my prince is gonna walk through those doors and rescue me from right behind the bar, you wait and see. I'm due for some mercy, so send him soon, Lord.'

"There were a few others, names I can't remember on account of their coming and going so fast, prompting new traveling dancers to squat for a spell. It was a small group working a small club, but it brought life to this little town, and now I was part of that.

"'Cover all the private parts, I'm coming in,' Jack warned before storming into the dressing room. 'I got a bachelor party paying admission as we speak. I want everyone back on the floor in five minutes if you want your job. Not ten. Not fifteen and a half. I'm handing out suspensions to all you lollygaggers. Also, I want to remind you all about the rules. Seems you all keep giving me a reason to have to repeat myself over and over. You bring any drugs into my club, unemployment will be the least of your worries. The zero-tolerance clause is still in full effect. There will be absolutely no brawling. You got a beef, you bring it to me or Harris. Last but not least, there will be no extra activities negotiated between you and my customers. We run a strip joint, not a whorehouse. You will sell drinks, you will sell conversation, you will sell dances, you will lie gracefully but you will not sell your body.'

"We all headed out single file, like the way you do when you're in elementary school. 'Are you scared?' Halo asked.

"'Is it that obvious?' I asked.

"'Yeah, it is, yellow belly,' Olive teased playfully. 'What kind of pills you like, uppers or downers? I got stuff to mellow you out if you need it.'

"'Uppers? Downers? What are those?' I asked.

"'Never mind,' Olive said.

"'I feel so out of place,' I confessed, tugging at my skirt, wishing it covered more skin.

"'Don't. We're all misfits. We never belong anywhere else either,' Halo said with a soft smile.

"Valentine hopped out of line to stand beside me. 'It's important that you don't let any of these girls intimidate you. I've got your back. Stick with me, and you'll be all right.'

"The first few months were way too easy. All financial gain and no immediate consequences that I knew of. It was simple: get on stage, parade around half-naked, and get paid a lot of money. The girls had finally warmed up to me. I was finding that inner strength Jack promised I would. With every stare, I felt more power. Customers bowed down to us, ready and willing to sip and swallow our venom if we ever gave them the chance. We were praised for our beauty and gallantry. I'm not ashamed to admit, it felt good. Attention had become my addiction. I'd soon discover that all of us had our own cross to bear.

"I was about four tequila shots in one night. I'd already had two sodas and an energy drink before that. Naturally, nature called. I politely excused myself from the table of tipsy tippers and made my way to the bathroom, bursting in, shoving my way into the first vacant stall. Only the one I shoved open wasn't as vacant as it appeared. There sat Valentine, face flushed, needle in her shoestring-tied arm.

"I stammered, 'Oh … I'm so sorry. I didn't know you were in here.'

"'It's okay, Mafia. I'm not embarrassed. Stay,' she mumbled, lethargic.

"'Okay.' I squatted.

"Valentine felt around until she found my hand and held it tight. A faint smile appeared, but so did a single tear, which confused me about what she was feeling. So I asked.

"'It feels like ice flooding the fire in my veins, flames triggered by the temper I gotta keep tamed, sadness planted inside that I harvest myself. At first it was nice, but now it's nothing but a bully to me, the need. The want. It dictates my whole life. And still I crave it, knowing I'm the battered woman in the relationship. Isn't that how it always works? We just keep coming on back for the same beating.'

"'You're in a relationship with your drugs?' I asked, trying hard to make sense of it all.

"'Oh yes. The needle, it's my longtime lover. It's the only one still here, that never left.'

"I looked at the floor, confused. It was the first time I'd seen the primal danger of what I'd gotten myself into. I wanted to hug Valentine, and maybe I should've.

"'To an addict like me, a drug dealer is God and the ten second fix is his blessing. Our decency is our sacrifice. Our bible is completely rewritten. The drug will drag you to submission; they don't tell you that up front. You gotta read the fine print, Mafia—never deal with anyone without asking about the catch. Walk, crawl, be dragged—regardless, you will submit. The few people who love addicts like me, they know the one true King, the one who made the heavens and the earth. We rely on you guys to relay our prayers, the prayers we're too sick to profess ourselves. You see, to an addict the devil is the memory of the heartache, all the bad times. It's the bad people we try to leave behind by getting high. Love will do you something vicious every time, way worse than the things hate can do. The devil is not a ghost or a man or a character, it's the thing that finally broke you. It's all the things in the closet.'

"Valentine licked her chapped lips and slowly blinked. 'You a good swimmer, Mafia?'

"It seemed like a peculiar question to ask out of the blue. 'Yeah, I'm a really good swimmer. I can do more than float.'

"'That's good. Half of life is just diving in. Nothing wrong with getting your feet wet, or just feeling free in the waves. But you can't go out too far. Don't go so far out that you can't see the shore, Mafia. Always know where home is. If you go too far out and get lost or run out of energy before you make it back, you might … drown. Promise me you'll never let the pain lead you out this far.'

"'I promise.' I held Valentine's hand for a while, watching the injection take over her body. She was smiling, but she was also still crying—odd, isn't it? 'Hey, Val, I was thinking, maybe we could all start praying together before we get on the floor to work, all of us as a group. Strength in numbers.'

"'I think that's a good idea, Mafia. You're a good girl. You stay that way; you hear me? Don't tell Jack about this. Believe it or not, management doesn't tolerate or support my habit, no matter how nice it makes me. They'll fire me for sure. I'm gonna shut my eyes for a minute, okay?'

"It didn't feel right, leaving Valentine there all alone, so frail. So I stayed. We did start pre-work prayer. I know it's the only thing that kept me safe night after night. Considering the ominous catastrophe that later took place at Club Malice, I can't help but think that maybe there was a weak link in the circle, one of us just spoke the prayer like a trained parakeet, never really let it into their heart. Said with lips but never imbedded in the heart. Maybe that's why the great perishing took place. Somebody wasn't praying right.

"I stuck with Valentine for a long time. I'd never met anyone so vivacious and free-spirited. I can remember watching her on stage, spinning and twirling, seeing the money being hurled in giant wads. In a strange way I admired her. It baffles me, even to this day, how Valentine and I reach the point of hatred. She'd always taken such good care of me, but then again, who could have foreseen what was coming?

"Maybe I should've walked away then, when I saw the very first sign of destruction. I should have. As I think back, I wonder, was it a sign from God? Did I stumble upon Valentine's meltdown for a reason? Was he trying to wake me up? It was scary, true, but not enough to send me fleeing. No, I stupidly ignored it. I convinced myself that I could handle being surrounded by such disorder; praying all the while that their demons would never pick a fight with me and triumph.

"Two years. Two years of my life were spent in the blink of eye. Time tends to fly when you move around in the night like the creatures we became. I had been drawn in by the glitter and kept safe by the fear of the cuts and bruises inflicted both mentally and physically on my fellow entertainers. Behind every steady smile that read *I'm in control* was a petrified little girl who just wanted to go home and be tucked in. Time was flying … many things had changed and some stayed the same in a bad way. Some friendships were strengthened, some weakened. Like Halo and me. We worked as a team most nights, dominating the stage together with matching Mardi Gras masks, to get the crowd hyped up. She and I had become best friends no matter how much she denied her need for a companion.

"The bond Valentine and I had shared was weakened to the point of detestation. Yeah, I hated her. I hated her to death. Everybody knew it."

Chapter 5

"I'd be telling a bald-faced lie if I said it didn't hurt, the bitter strife between Valentine and me. I'd grown to care for her, depend on her guidance. I remember the dead stares we shared whenever we were in the dressing room together. It was ravenous, the anger. I used to say I could never hold a grudge. I wasn't raised that way. But you'd be surprised what you're capable of when you're hurt that badly.

"I was different, after those two years. I'd grown up. I found myself giving thanks on a daily basis, thankful that I never had to do anything other than dance to make ends meet. There are a million ways to make money in dark places. Somehow I stayed in the light, focused on the reason I was there. Focused on achieving my dreams and some of the people I worked with—my boss and a few select dancers kept me as safe as possible, naïve to the things I didn't need to see. I was making money, a lot of it. But even on nights when there was so much money that I would nod off while counting, I wasn't happy. I wasn't fulfilled. Sometimes I'd stack it all up and just stare it, angry at the money for some reason. Thinking, *How can people be so frivolous? Waste all this cash?* There would be days when I'd shut myself off from everyone: family, friends, work friends, managers, everyone. I'd sit in my room for days with the lights off and blankets strung over the windows to keep the sun out, just staring at the profit, deeply depressed. The most days I ever spent inside depressed like that? Eight. I don't even think I ate. No, just occasional sips of water to make up for the tears that poured out.

"'What are you doing here? You don't even smoke, goody two-shoes,' January teased.

"'Just waiting on the sunset to fall hard. Have you ever seen it coming down over the tracks? Magnificent. It really is.'

"'Yeah, it's kinda pretty, Peaceful to watch I guess, if you're trying to free your mind.'

"'Indeed.'

"'Glad I got you alone, been worried about you since the High-Rise incident. You've been sullen, distant from us all. You and Valentine still not speaking?'

"'I don't have anything to say her, January. I hope you didn't come back here to try to plead her case or play the mediator. Some bridges are meant to be burned.'

"'I know you're upset. Hell, I don't blame you one bit. Take your time on the healing part, but not the forgiving part. Everyone deserves forgiveness. It's a birthright, you know ...'

"'I can't even look at her.'

"'Maybe not today,' January said, puffing on her cigarette.

"'Maybe not ever.'

"'You don't mean that, sugar.'

"'I might ...'

"'We all mess up.'

"I turned to January and squinted. 'You sure are unusually zen today.'

"'I've got my reasons,' she said, beaming. 'Take a look at this.' She fiddled around in her purse and handed me a slip of paper.

"My heart just about jumped out of my chest as I looked at the ultrasound. 'You're pregnant! I'm so happy for you!'

"'I was just about to give up hope, and then I couldn't keep my junk food from coming back up. Went in praying it wasn't the stomach flu and walked out with that ultrasound for a keepsake. Imagine that. I'm so ... I'm so ...' January began to cry.

"I pulled her close. 'Why are you crying?'

"'Because I can't ...'

"'Can't what?'

"'Can't be happy. Not yet.'

"'Why not?'

"''Cause nothing that makes me this happy can last. Something's going to go wrong, I just know it. Who am I to get everything I've ever wanted?'

"'January, you can't think like that. You should be happy right now—tears of joy and happiness.'

"'I can't, on account of all the things that could go wrong.'

"I held the ultrasound close to her face. 'Do you see this? Look at it. This is a blessing. Maybe you can't be happy because you think you don't deserve this, but you do. I want you to do something for me. Turn that worry into a prayer. Kiss this little photo every day and every night. Look at it whenever you get scared. Look at how precious this little life is. God is trusting you to keep this child safe and sound for nine whole months in that belly. You think stress is *good* for the baby?'

"'He is precious, isn't he?'

"'He? It's a little early to tell, isn't it?' I asked, studying the grainy snapshot for male parts.

"'Well, it just feels like a boy.'

"'We'll have to wait and see, won't we? Any names in mind?'

"'Not yet. Dale is dead-set on a junior, but I'll find a way around that.'

"We both laughed, hugging, staring at the picture together. 'For now, we'll just call him little piglet.'

"'Okay. Hi, little piglet,' she whispered sweetly. 'We can't wait to meet you. Momma's got a lot of hot girls waiting to hold you.'

"Jack kicked open the back door and walked toward the two of us, sparking a cigarette. 'What's this? A Girl Scout reunion? Let me guess, you got a fresh batch of thin mints to sell?' he snapped.

"'Oh, Jack, how I've grown to love that bland sense of humor of yours,' January said. 'Not even you can stifle my joy today,' she added, smiling at me.

"'Joy? What you got to be so happy about?'

"'Nothing,' she replied, pursing her lips.

"Jack stepped closer and eyed January for a minute before stepping back and tilting his head to the side, as if thinking. 'You're looking extra bright today. Dare I say you're glowing.'

"'Am I?'

"'Yeah.' He puffed some more and then gave her a pat on the shoulder. 'Congratulations. Don't think I'm gonna cut you any slack around here,' he said with a smirk. 'Soon as you start showing, you're on door duty checking IDs and cashing in big bills, sitting in a chair where nobody can see how fat you're going to get. Can't have folks giving me the evil eye for having a prego on her feet all night, understood?'

"'Understood. You think we could keep this just between us for now?'

"'Jack don't pillow talk, you know that,' he said, referring to himself in the third person as he did whenever he chose to state a fact about himself. 'Your secret's safe with me,' he promised with a wink. 'Go on in now. You make this your last cigarette break until you have that baby, you hear? Darn thing gonna come out with an extra ear or something. Go on in, get to work. Money don't make itself.'

"After January went inside, Jack sat beside me. 'Heard about the High-Rise incident. I wanna let you know I'll deal with Valentine in the harshest manner possible. This makes the club look bad and I won't stand for it. I'm disappointed in her. People already hate this kind of establishment. I can't keep these girls from freelancing, but it gives the business a bad name, makes us all look guilty by association. Has people thinking we encourage this type of behavior. Truth is, it sickens us most of all. One bad apple ... she knows better. Day by day she's slowly slipping away. Can you believe she used to be sweet on me?' Jack asked, shaking his head.

"'But that was way back when she still had that spark. Way back before her body started telling on her, with the weight loss and tooth decay. Wish I would've caught it early on, maybe could've helped her. It happens. Some of us have one or two demons on our back. That poor girl, she's got an army. When you're ready to talk about it, my door is always open for you.'

"'I appreciate that, Jack, but I'm not ready.'

"'Figured you wouldn't be. Too soon. I get it. Just ... whenever you're ready, find a shoulder to lean on and not a substance.'

"Jack headed back inside, but I stayed out back a while longer. January was right. I hadn't been the same, and unlike witnessing drug use or being caught right smack dab in the middle of a drunken club scuffle, I couldn't just pretend to not see or bandage the ache away. There was some form of mental mutilation done inside me that made me colder than I was before. I know now that damage is irreversible;

it's not going anywhere. Sometimes all you can expect is a scar, no healing. Angry wives who can't figure out why their husbands would rather have us warm their laps than be nagged to the point of madness, demeaning belittlement, being called everything except your rightful name, the stress and worry of an unprofitable night, unjustified police harassment and more—this was my world now."

Diana interrupted. "High-Rise incident? What is that? What happened?"

"We'll get there, Diana. We'll get there."

Chapter 6

"It's priceless, the look on people's faces when they ask what you do for a living and you reply, 'I dance.'

"'So you're a ballerina or a choreographer?' they ask.

"Then you see that fearful hope arise, praying you don't say the word *exotic*. You know, of all the stereotypes I hate, the notion that we became dancers because we were once molested or sexually abused is the one I hate the most. 'You poor thing! Was it a twisted uncle or a trusted family friend?' Why do they always tilt their head to the side and gently rub your forearm? Is that supposed to make the question seem mildly appropriate?

"Imagine hating that assumption but having that shoe fit, in your case. Then you just have to sit there with a hard mug, incapable of objection. Yeah, I was seven when I was forced to abandon my virtue, the result of revolting desire. It wasn't an uncle or a neighborhood playground camper. It was a cousin from out of state who came down to the country to vacation with us each summer. He was older and loved to nap with us because that meant he got to get under a blanket with us. The things he did when it was naptime … one time my aunt walked in and he was so arrogant that he didn't even take his hand out of my pants. And as I watched her walk around the room collecting the dirty laundry, I prayed she'd snatch the sheet off us to put in her basket and see what he was doing. I wanted to scream but I didn't.

"It wasn't just me; it happened to a few others in my family, all of us around the same age. Once we were older, we talked about it. The weird part, none of us can remember why we were so afraid to say something to our parents. He'd never threatened us outright. Maybe it made us feel that dirty, that we felt like we'd done something wrong.

After something like that happens, you tend to look at the world differently.

"But that had nothing to do with me becoming a dancer. No, I had way more things wrong with me back then, and I wasn't ready to accept or confess or change those things. It's never just one thing that makes us hate ourselves. One thing isn't enough. I'm not the only flower plucked before its time. I worked side by side with women who were once victims of a pervert's appetite. A girl I once worked with told me that after she'd been touched and robbed of hope, she stopped looking for God. She said she could remember it happening, asking God to come but he didn't show up. I couldn't relate. I was never that confused, to give up on God or ask him to give up on me. But I recognized the look in her lost angel eyes. Those eyes used to be mine. Most people will measure your strength by how much you can endure without bending or breaking, and that's not fair. Those things we pretend never happened can make you do bad things. You gotta get those things prayed straight out of you as soon as possible. The longer they sit, the harder those demons are to shake.

"Dancing for me was a choice, as unladylike as that is to admit. I made a conscious decision to parade naked for financial gain, but not all of us were blessed with a choice. Not everyone who dances *wants* to. Some are forced to strip as slaves in this industry. Forced by men, lowlife individuals who lack basic human decency. These degenerates seek women with the lowest self-esteem and poor work ethic. They sift the gutter for the ones who had very little positive influence and education. They can't do anything with women who can think for themselves; it's too difficult to break them. They need them weak, already broken. They need them hopeless with no one to call on. Those are the ones they feel are built to receive their misguidance."

"Forgive me if I'm reading this all wrong, but are you talking about pimps?" Diana asked from the edge of her seat.

"Yes, Diana, I'm talking about pimps, men who assist with and/or manipulate the steep negotiation of sexual companionship for a sum of money. Never mind the hideous peacock hat and the cheap ivory hand-me-down Easter Sunday suit. Those are just animations, poor inaccurate caricatures drawn up by the idea of modern-day businessmen moving product. These monsters are as real as the thick, uncomfortable air between you and me. You can find them in any gentleman's club, not necessarily welcomed but there. To the untrained eye they can be hard to spot, but for someone who's weathered the lifestyle for a few years, it' quite easy. They usually sit at the bar inconspicuously mimicking the mannerisms of an ordinary paying customer, sipping the same drink at midnight that they bought at six. They may banter with the others sitting at the bar or toss the occasional dollar to throw management off their scent, but make no mistake, they're working, watching their merchandise."

"Merchandise? What do you mean? Whores?"

"I know this is your set and all, but please adjust your nomenclature. I don't like who I become when I get angry. Being offended makes me angry. I call them friends. Unkind people call them whores."

"I'm sorry … that was discourteous of me."

"It's okay. My friends you reference, they're sufferers, and sufferers tend to be generous with their forgiveness. The ignorant know not what they do."

Diana sipped her lukewarm tea, as if to pass the awkwardness, before continuing. "So you encountered pimps during your time at Club Malice?"

"Oh yes. I'd even been approached by three or four but was never charmed by their pipe dreams for a brighter tomorrow. I've heard it all: *I can teach you how to make triple what you're making now. With your body and my hustle plan, you can retire in five years. What you need is somebody like me, someone who can put you up on game.* Yeah, they're real slick with their approach, but I took God with me to work every night. Yeah, God goes to places like that too. My money was dirty enough from just stripping. I didn't need it filthy. There's a fine line between dancing and prostitution, and I never crossed it. Unfortunately, I lost a few friends that way. I thank God that I was never that lost, that gullible, that alone.

"But Olive wasn't as strong-willed as the rest of us. It had been a slow week at the club. Holiday season makes very little spending money for the average family man. I'd been in the back for more than an hour, killing time, reading. Olive burst in, late for the fifth time that month.

"I greeted her casually. 'Hey, Olive. Steer clear of Jack. He swears he's suspending you on sight. Make up something good. I'm thinking death in the family. Gonna take something serious to get him off your case this time. I saved the obituary section for you. Take your pick from the list of stiffs and pretend to be devastated.'

"I'd looked over at her but she didn't say hello back or react to anything. It was as if she didn't hear me at all. She always said hello back, but that night she seemed bothered, distressed. I eyed her inquisitively as she franticly fingered through her locker.

"'Hey, you okay?' I asked, walking over. She was still quiet. I placed my hand on her back. 'Olive, sweetie, what's wrong?'

"'I can't find my black garter! It's gone!'

"'A garter? Is that all? It's okay, I have a white one you borrow for tonight.'

"'No! I need a black one! If it's not black it'll clash my whole outfit and then I won't look presentable. If I'm not presentable I won't make money, and if I don't make money—'

"I grabbed her wrist to stop her from digging, demanding she acknowledge me. 'Olive, stop! What will happen if you don't make money?'

"'Tosh.'

"'Tosh? Who's Tosh? And what exactly is he going to do?'

"Before she could tell me anything, it was time for her to perform. I heard the announcement: 'Next up, we got Olive coming to the main stage!'

"'Do you want me to tell Saddle you're not ready?'

"'No! I gotta get up there. I just have to!'

"While Olive danced, I peeked out from behind the curtain, scanning the bar. One patron stood out from the others. He was watching Olive but not the way the other men did. He eyed her the way a coach observed a player, as if to critique and criticize. When Olive's set was over, his face hardened like concrete. The stage was penniless. Not one person had tipped. And you could tell he was dissatisfied.

"At closing, Olive had only made a measly seven dollars, not counting the handful of nickels tossed on stage as a cruel joke executed by a childish heckler who'd just turned eighteen, as if to say she wasn't attractive enough for a full dollar.

"After I dressed, I noticed Olive at the bar with her head hung low. I reached into my purse and approached her, tapping her on the shoulder.

'Olive, you've got to be more mindful. You dropped this hundred dollar bill. I just found it here on the floor next to your stool. It must've fallen out of your pocket when you sat down.'

"She looked up at me like I was an angel. She knew it was impossible, the money belonging to her, which meant I was lying because I wanted to help her out. Olive tried to speak, but I feared her pride would compromise her blessing. I couldn't let her turn it down.

"'You're welcome,' I interrupted. 'Just be glad *I* found it and not somebody else. Not everyone's as honest, you know.'

"I slid the cash into her hand and clutched it for a moment. 'I don't have much, but I do have a couch. It's yours if you ever need shelter, a safe place.'

Chapter 7

"It makes me mad when I hear people say, 'Women are emotional creatures.' But this is true. Life just affects us differently, and our phases morph differently. We tend to hold onto pain longer than men because most things that bring us pain also make us sad. Sadness has a stubborn way of getting comfortable in our spirits. We walk around with it, unaware of how it's affecting our personalities.

"Thank God for Friday night customers with electronic payroll deposits. It was the first good night we'd had in a while, and tensions were running high alongside eagerness. There had been a drought drying up the club. It happens like clockwork every year. Men tend to treat their wives and children to gifts at Christmas instead of treating themselves to trouser arousals, but that night was finally lucrative. Every glass was full. Every lap was warm. Money was flowing, both cash and debit cards being passed back and forth over the bar.

"I sat at the vanity touching up my makeup. Jack burst into the dressing quarters, causing all the slackers to stir. 'Mafia, where the hell is Valentine? Saddle's called her to the stage four times already! I got music playing and no one dancing! I sure as hell ain't getting up there in a thong! The crowds getting restless! What's she trying to do, ruin me?'

"'Who knows where she ran off to this time? Who cares? I'm not her keeper? She's not in my pocket. My advice—put tracking devices on all the stragglers like wild dogs since they roam around like vagrant mutts,' I snapped.

"'Look, I know the two of you still have some personal issues to hash out, but this here is business. A business I bust my ass to keep afloat so you all can have a place to make an honest living. She's still got a job to do, kids to feed, and I still got a club to run. Now get up, get rid of the attitude, and go find her. Tell her I said to check in with Saddle at the DJ booth. I need full rotation tonight, no stage pauses. Don't do it for her, do it for me. You haven't let me down yet, so don't start now. And don't roll your eyes, I see everything.'

"I rolled my eyes anyway when he was gone, but I did as I was told. I scanned the VIP section. I checked the lap dance foyer. I looked in the men's and the women's bathrooms.

"I grabbed my coat and wandered into the parking lot. 'Hey, any of you guys seen Valentine?' All I got was blank faces and shrugs. The only place I hadn't looked was the tracks in the back where the smokers went on break. It was then that I witnessed a strange man emerge from behind the club. He saw me and his guilty beady eyes shifted to the ground almost immediately.

"'Hey! Hey you! I'm looking for my coworker Valentine. Have you seen her tonight?'

"He didn't answer.

"'Caucasian girl? Her hair is light brown and long, curly. She's tall …'

"He never answered, just quickly hopped into his pickup and peeled off.

"'I'll take that as a no!' I yelled. 'How rude.'

"Suddenly the ground trembled. I took a few steps into the darkness and looked down the tracks. I could see blinking lights. A train was coming. I stepped into the night a bit more.

"'Valentine! Valentine, you back here? Look, Jack is really pissed. You'd better get inside and dance your set!'

"I heard a cough between the train whistle's rhythmic pattern. I pulled my phone from my pocket and used it for light. 'Valentine, I don't have time for this crap! You think I care if you get fired?'

"Then I saw her in the distance, lying on her stomach face-down directly across the tracks. I looked to my left and panicked as I calculated the distance between the train and Valentine's body. 'Oh my God,' I muttered, blood running ice cold in my veins.

"I ran as fast as I could, yelling, praying she would hear me and get up. 'Val! The train!' I screamed. 'Get up!'

"But she was still. I made it to her side and shook her, screaming her name.

"She tried to speak, but I couldn't understand what she was trying to say. Her mouth was white and foamy on the outer corners. Her eyes were twitchy and blinking. The intense vibrations of the rushing locomotive began to scramble the contents of my stomach. I looked up and realized we were quickly running out of time.

"'Wait! Please stop!' I yelled, waving my arms in the bright light. It was a waste of energy. Even if they could see us, they'd never be able to stop in time. The sound of the train on the steel sounded like nails across a chalkboard. I knew I needed to act. The train was rapidly rushing right for us, and I was afraid but knew what I had to do.

"I grabbed Valentine's wrists tight and began to pull. At first she barely budged. I began to pray. My strength was limited, and I knew only God could help me. I also knew she wasn't going to die alone—I wasn't going to just leave her. I'd decided either we would both live or both die. I prayed, *God please give me the strength to save her, save us both. Or give me the bravery to die trying.* I pulled. I pulled again. Still nothing. I panicked and sobbed.

"'God, please!' That time I felt it deep in my belly, the plea. I pulled again, and miraculously that time it worked.

"I dragged her from the tracks and out of the train's path. Just in the nick of time, I cleared her ankles from the rails. I felt the wind from the train roaring. I don't think I breathed again until it passed completely, and then I sat shaking.

"I looked down at Valentine and pulled her near. 'We're going to get it all out, okay?' I turned her head to the side and shoved my fingers far down her throat.

"She gagged. Warm charcoal colored bile, food chunks and pill casings poured out all over my hand.

"Valentine gasped, coughing and shivering.

"'It's going to be okay now.' I tried to lift her again to bring her inside, but she was too heavy to carry. We fell back down, so I positioned her head comfortably in my lap. I took off my coat and covered her so she wouldn't be cold. She was in and out of consciousness.

"I knew there was a slim chance she'd remember anything I had to say but I spoke to her anyway. 'They'll come looking for us. They'll notice we're missing and come find us and then we'll get you inside where it's warm. I won't leave you. I'll stay with you just this once, okay? Doesn't change anything, the way I feel. Make no mistake, I'm still furious.'

"She lightly squeezed my arm, as if to say, 'Yes, I know you're here and I thank you.'

"'Who did this to you? Who's selling to you? Can't they see you've had enough? Is this not enough? I think you're more dead than alive. One foot in the grave already … maybe you're begging for more … maybe death is the point of it all for you. Valentine, I'm going to stay with you, keep you from freezing to death tonight, but I need you to know that this is it. Our friendship, it's over. In fact, I don't wanna know you at all. First the high-rise, now this. I want you to be a stranger from here on out. You and I are gonna work together, but we can't be friends anymore. You're on your way down. You're sinking. You know it. I know you know it. I just can't swim for us both anymore. I'll never stop praying for you, but we just can't know each other anymore. We're not friends.'

"I felt her squeeze again, and she held on a little longer than before. Sleet began to fall in the twilight, small pieces of soft ice, closet thing to snow I'd ever seen in the south. I remember how cold it got sitting there rocking her, making sure she stayed warm. I cried the whole time, which made my cheeks even colder. No one found us out back until dawn. Even if I had yelled, there's no way they would have heard me over the music. My lips were nearly numb after five hours of waiting to be rescued. My face felt ceramic.

"'What the hell, Mafia! You trying to die of pneumonia?' Halo asked.

"'Better than drowning,' I replied, shivering.

"'What's wrong with her?' Halo asked, wrapping me in a sweater as we watched Harris and Jack carry Valentine back into the club.

"'She swam out too far.'

"'What?' Halo asked, confused.

"'She can't see the shore no more,' I answered.

Chapter 8

"Have you ever been shattered? Dented to the point where you feel like you can't even summon the strength to pray? Like if you got on your knees you wouldn't have the energy to get back up and would just die on the floor. Maybe because God told you which way to go and you didn't listen the first time. So now you're too ashamed to pray about it a second time 'cause that would mean admitting you were wrong about everything you thought you knew."

"Once or twice. What about you?" Diana countered.

"Oh yes. Too many times to count, actually. Yeah, I know a thing or two about pain. We all did. In fact, we were experts on the subject."

"A drunk Sage yelled from behind the bar, 'Men are filthy creatures! Disgusting! I hate 'em all: big men, small men, overcompensating men. I even hate male toddlers because they grow up to be men!' The club had only been open for forty-five minutes and she was already sloshed, reeling from her latest breakup.

"'Sage! I told you to stay out of the Courvoisier and I mean it! That's for big spenders only! You know how much we charge a glass for that watered-down crap, you're the one doing the pouring. I'll send you home for the night and dock your pay!' Jack yelled from the office.

"'Shut up! I ain't been in the liquor! I brought this from home!' she fired back, pulling up her loose bra strap.

"'I'll suspend you! I will!' he threatened again.

"'Oh shut up …' Sage muttered, nearing the end of the bar where I sat reading eighteenth-century love poetry.

"She snatched the book from my grasp. 'Reading up on love, are we? Don't bother. Life ain't nothing but a long bad romance, trust me, I know. Mafia, promise me. I want you to promise me that you'll never fall in love with someone you meet in this dump! They're no good. You can't expect to find a good man in a place where they don't believe they can find a good woman. They're just hungry and desperate or bored at home, out of options. They'll do anything! Say anything to get what they hunger for,' she ranted, slurring every other word and pausing for sips of brown liquor.

"'And what are they hungry for?' I asked, creasing my lips tight to hide the fact that I found her drunken rant slightly amusing.

"'What do you think? They hunger for you! Your attention! The very essence of youth. They want the idea of you, a fantasy they can replay for kicks and giggles. They wanna show your pictures and private intimate recordings to their impotent unemployed friends to make themselves seem superior. It's all just for sick fun!' She smashed her glass on the bar top. It shattered but she barely noticed, just sipped from the bottle instead.

"'Don't go tearing up my bar, Sage! You're pushing it tonight!' Jack threatened again.

"'Ain't nobody tearing up nothing, Jack! Don't have a payroll to cheat us on back there!'

"'He sounds serious, Sage. Maybe you've had enough for tonight,' I reasoned, attempting to take the bottle from her grasp.

"She jerked away hard. 'Don't try and cut me off when I'm trying to share my wisdom! It's disrespectful! Now, where was I? Oh right, men and the fun they have. It's not fun for us, Mafia. Such dangerous lusts holding us captive, locked up with every hug. Chained away with every kiss. The aftermath, what's left over, it's not fun to be haunted by. Once all the great fun is had, there's only pain. Worst part, you'll think you're having the time of your life until you wake up one day and stare at a lonely middle-aged single mom in the mirror instead of your usual beautiful familiar reflection. A game, it's all a game and only the tricksters win. What makes her so great? Huh? The girl before me or after me? What makes her worthy of all of him? What makes me so misfortunate that I got the worst parts of him? And let him know daily that it's enough for me? Because I love all of him, even the ugly parts.'

"'Tricksters?'

"'Yes, stupid girl, tricksters! Keep up! The ones who know that nothing they're promising will come to pass but lead you on anyway in such a believable fashion. Professional liars, they are. And they say we're the ones selling dreams by distracting them with our half-naked bodies. Collateral damage, that's what we are. Opened hearts in the wrong place at the wrong time and we accidentally crossed paths with the devil. And the heartbreakers, they see your pain as a way in, not as a chance to right the last man's wrongdoing. They just wanna add to the ruins, leave you wondering what you could have possibly done to deserve such an emotional ass beating. I know I'm drunk, but I'm telling you this because I love you. I want you to know that,' she slurred, falling of the barstool, dragging the cash register down with her.

"'That's it! You're going home for the night! Harris, get her out of here, put her in a cab and make sure they don't make any stops, straight home! I want you back up here at opening tomorrow, sober and extremely apologetic!'

"'I ain't leaving! Go to hell, Jack!'

"'Stop resisting, Sage!" Harris yelled. He desperately tried to fend off Sage's scratching and biting.

"I laughed. Harris was the biggest giant I'd ever seen. No matter who his opponent was, I always put my money on him, but he took a loss that night. Sage kicked his ass the entire way out of the club. I guess muscle is no match for a drunken, heartbroken stripper scorned.

"Contrary to common belief, entertainers do work during the week. We don't hibernate Monday through Thursday and wake up on Friday ready to party like groupies fueled on caffeine and tequila. No, were not *that* deadbeat and indolent. We set alarms to wake up on time just like regular joes. We're expected to keep a certain standard of hygiene. We groom and dress appropriately to suit the environment. We show up complaining about how tired we are just like everybody else in the working class and we produce the very same determined work ethic. We hustle just as hard on Sunday nights as we do on Saturday nights. Sure we take every other holiday off; we aren't machines, but we work hard. Make no mistake, we had bank accounts to fill. Yes, strippers have bank accounts as well as savings accounts. We can read too—that might be surprising to some folks.

"It's a nice thought, only working on the weekends, but the money is way easier to make on a weekday. The men who stop in on their way home or the ones who are supposed to be at the grocery store buying milk, they know what they want. They want to ogle beautiful women, and they know they don't have all night to get the mental pix they need to go home to their stale wives who no longer go the extra mile to make themselves desirable. Weekday customers understand that our attention is phony and the level of comfort we can provide is limited in terms of pleasure. They know there's no chance for intimacy, no possibility of a relationship developing, sexual or casual. Why else would they ask our names and accept our stage alias? Deep down they know it's not real. No matter how hard they try to convince themselves otherwise, they know what's real and what isn't once they return to their lives outside of the club. Weekdays, that's when the most put-together individuals stop in.

"It was a typical uneventful Tuesday that I met him."

"Him?" Diana asked.

"Princeton."

"Is he the love interest in your story?"

"No, he's nothing but the love of my life.

"It was steady money for a Tuesday night. No one in the building would have been considered a millionaire, but they all had company cards and salaries. I, the social butterfly, mingled, shaking hands and sparking small talk with the regulars.

"'Hey, Mafia! You tired?' Percy asked, setting up the same textbook pickup line he used nightly.

"'If I say yes, and you say I've been running through your mind all day, I'm gonna kick you out of my club,' I joked.

"It's funny now that I think back on it. You see, I planned to pass Princeton by. At first sight I was intrigued and can honestly admit he was handsome, but in a wholesome way. It's rare, stumbling upon a gentleman in a gentlemen's club, no strip clubs facilitate dogs. I knew he was different the very first time I laid eyes on him, but I wasn't going to spark up a conversation. I was shy and knew he could do better than me. I was nothing but a stripper with a dream of becoming a famous writer.

"He held out his hand, blocking my path. 'Hello.' Kindness in fair simplicity, but it was more than enough.

41

"'Hi,' I replied.

"He stood there for a minute, not speaking. I panicked a bit, wondering what could he be thinking. Was my breath foul? Was I not as pretty up close? But then he smiled, big. And against my best efforts, I blushed.

"'What's your name?'

"'Mafia,' I replied, holding out my hand.

"He stepped closer, taking my hand in his. 'No it's not.'

"'Excuse me?'

"'That's not your name,' he whispered with a grin.

"'And how do you know that? It could be. I could have a birth certificate at home that reads just that.'

"'But you don't. No self-respecting mother would name her child Mafia.'

"'Okay, maybe you're right, but you're still not getting my real name.'

"'Fair enough.'

"'You can tell me your name though.'

"'It's Princeton.'

"'Is that a fake name to one-up my stage name?'

"'No, that's my real, corny name. Princeton Cambridge.'

"'Your name is Princeton Cambridge? You're named after two exclusive universities?'

"'Yeah. My mother, also self-respecting, obviously had a sense of humor. I never lived up to either school's standards. I'm just an average guy.'

"'Somehow I doubt that.'

"We'd began to smile again, and I knew I had to walk away. He was far too charming and it made me nervous. 'Well, it was nice to meet you.'

"'Where are you going?'

"'If you must know, my day job shift starts in three hours.'

"'Day job? How many jobs do you have?'

"'I got myself two jobs and a dream, so three if you're keeping count.'

"'Ambitious too. I like that.'

"'Well, I'm flattered, but I really must be going.'

"'I can't let you leave yet.'

"'Why not?'

"Princeton leaned in for an intimate whisper, and his face grew more serious. 'Because I was hoping you'd help me out with a little problem I'm having.'

"'Problem?'

"'You see, I'm a grown man who's never had a private dance from a beautiful woman.'

"It was complete bull, I knew. 'Oh really? Never had a lap dance?'

"'Never. In fact, this is my first time in a topless bar.'

"'Well that's a shame. I'm sorry to hear that,' I said, my sympathy purposely fake and excessively dramatic.

"'My sentiments exactly, but if you're really truly sorry, you'd exalt me with a dance.'

"'You have expensive taste, Mr. Cambridge.'

"'That I do. So what do you say? One dance? Please. Have some pity on me?'

"I obliged, but at every song's end, he'd buy another and another. I lost count after the ninth or tenth song. 'You know, you're quite comfortable for a man who's never been on the receiving end of a lap dance before.'

"'Maybe you just make it easy for a man to feel comfortable.'

"'Or maybe you're lying about never being in a strip club.'

"'Okay, you got me. I've been to a few. Some far nicer, but I wasn't lying about the dance part.'

"'You expect me to believe you've been to clubs and never got a dance?'

"'No, I expect you to believe that none of the other women were beautiful.'

"It was smooth, and I found myself immersed in flattery for the second time since we'd met. It was flirtation and I knew it. I deferred the conversation and ended the session. 'Sir, it's been fun, but it's time for me to go now. I hope you've enjoyed your entertainment.'

"'Do you really have to go?' he asked, clearly disappointed.

"'Yes. And you should leave too, before you spend your retirement fund,' I teased while dressing.

"'Well, I hope you met your quota for the night.'

"'I have now,' I said with a wink.

"'At the risk of sounding like your typical barfly, can I have your number?'

"'Four … eight.'

"'That's only two numbers.'

"'I know. I'm usually here four nights a week for no more than eight hours a night, the minimum shift requirement. This isn't a career, Mr. Cambridge.'

"'Okay, I'll be sure to remember that. But I meant your phone number.'

"'I'll tell you what. We'll play Rumpelstiltskin for it. Since you're so certain my real name isn't Mafia, guess what it really is. You ever guess my real name correctly, I'll gladly give you my number. You have my word.'

"Princeton laughed hysterically, and I was puzzled. 'That won't be too hard,' he said arrogantly.

"I'd turned to walk away. 'Let me know when you think you got it, okay?'

"'Sure thing, Reese,' he said proudly, haughtily.

"I stopped and slowly turned around, slightly shocked and defeated.

"He strolled over with his phone in hand, smile bold enough to stretch from ear to ear. Princeton placed the phone in my fist. 'You can go on ahead and put your info in. You can still save it under Mafia in the contact list if you want, but I'm never gonna call you that. Your real name is prettier, I think. It's less scary too.'

"I snatched the phone and saved my number. 'When you call, I'll be sure to save your number under Officer Cambridge.'

"'How'd you know I'm a cop?'

"'Well … you smell like bacon of course …'

"'Oh really?' he asked, laughing.

"I leaned in. 'No, not really. I felt your badge digging into my backside the entire time I was grinding on you. You're either a cop or extremely satisfied with your lap dance purchase.'

"Princeton watched me walk away and finished his beer. 'Before you go? What's your dream?'

"'I want to become a writer one day. I want to write love stories and novels that make people fall in love with literature again.'

"'That's an honest dream. I hope it comes true.'

"'Well, that's the plan.'

"A cop who knew my name seemed like nothing at the time. Most people just match names to local faces on social media. Some customers overhear dancers talking to other dancers accidentally using government names. Either way, his profession mattered very little at the time. I had nothing to hide, so there was nothing to be afraid of. I still don't have anything to hide."

Chapter 9

"'Look what got delivered! Someone has a secret admirer,' Whisper said, barging into the dressing room, approaching my side with a large crystal vase of flowers, handing them over to me.

"'What's all this?' I asked, sincerely surprised.

"'Don't know. Someone left them at the bar for you. Open the card! Read it! Read it!'

"Saw these and thought they were beautiful—naturally they made me think of you.

"'How sweet! You didn't tell me you were seeing anyone, Mafia! Since when do we keep secrets this juicy?'

"'Technically I'm not seeing him. We just talk on the phone every now and then. Sometimes we catch a bite to eat when I get off. It's no big deal, really.'

"'It certainly looks like a big deal to me,' Whisper said, smelling the flowers before slinking out of the dressing room with a girlish smirk.

"I'd lied. It was a big deal.

"'Hey, Mafia, January needs you. She's in the bathroom having a maximum-level meltdown. Might wanna bring her a tampon before she turns the club into the red river,' Olive teased with a cruel childish laugh.

"Rolling my eyes, annoyed by her unnecessary high school teasing, I answered, 'Yeah, sure thing, I'll bring her one.'

"Thinking nothing of it at the time, I got up, headed to my locker to retrieve the feminine product, but then stopped. *Tampon? Why would January need that? She's pregnant ...*

"'Well ... are you gonna go before she floods the building and runs off all the customers?' Olive asked, curiously eyeing my hesitation.

"'Yeah. I said I got it, relax.' I walked into the bathroom, allowing my eyes to adjust to the foggy dimness rectified by the occasional flicker of the defective high-frequency fluorescent lights poorly installed overhead.

"Pushing my way past two new dancers whose names I never bothered asking, I made my way to January, who sat near the last stall on the left with her legs folded inward, chin resting on her knees.

"I kneeled down, placing my hand on her shoulder. 'Sweetie, why are you on the floor? What's the matter?' I asked before I noticed the blood smeared between the inside of her upper thighs.

"'It's gone, Mafia.'

"'What's gone?'

"'Little piglet.'

"'What do you mean *gone*?'

"'It's in there,' she muttered, stretching her arm out, pointing behind me to the first stall in the restroom.

"I turned back, eyeing the out-of-order warning scribbled in permanent marker on a solid piece of loose-leaf paper. 'It's in there,' she mumbled again, sadder the second time.

"I stood, took a deep breath, and slowly moved toward the stall. With my fingertips, I pushed it open, stepping inside. My heart stopped and I covered my mouth as if to seal in the scream before it alarmed anyone else. I gasped and slammed the stall door shut.

"'Everybody out!'

"The stragglers ceased their conversation and looked at me with raised brows. It occurred to me that they hadn't heard of me.

"'Look, your blood can stay in your veins or it can spill out on the floor, makes no difference to me. I'll say it once more. Get out!' I yelled, jostling all the occupants, locking January and me inside.

"I ran back to January's side. 'What happened?' I yelled, clutching her tight.

"'I deserve it. My womb really is a vile pit. I'm poisonous to my own seed.'

"'No. You didn't deserve this.'

"'Didn't I? If I weren't trash, would this be happening? If God loved me, would he take away my gift to create life, a chance to do a better job than my momma ever did?'

"'God *does* love you, January.'

"'And this is how he shows me…?'

"I didn't know what to say so I shut up for a minute. We just sat there hugging on a filthy floor covered in dirty mop streaks. Wasn't long before the herd of full bladders came, banging.

"'Open up! I gotta pee! Unlock the door!'

"I ignored them. 'January, I know you're hurting, but this is not the time or the place to break down. Come, let me get you out of here.'

"'No!'

"'I'm not gonna just leave you bleeding on the floor, January!'

"'I'm not leaving him here!' she declared defiantly with enraged eyes not blinking. 'I made him. And now what is he? Medical waste? Fecal matter to just be plunged and flushed? No! He was my baby and he existed. He's real. I'm not leaving him.'

"'I know; I understand …'

"'No! You don't.'

"It was true. I didn't understand. I was never a mother, not even for a second. And the fact that I'd said it knowing there's no way I could feel what she was feeling made me like a bad friend.

"The banging on the door got louder. I could tell by the thickness of the roar that more had gathered outside. Hanging at January's side was a purple and gold Crown Royal pouch that dancers used to keep money and personal belongings safe. The gold shimmering rope made for a handy tie around January's wrist. I loosened the pouch free, emptying its contents— lip balm, some gum, and a cigarette lighter—onto the floor. I ran back to the out-of-order stall and stepped inside again. The stench of fresh vomit turned my stomach, but what I saw was much worse than any smell. In the toilet, below the worn stained porcelain rim right above a cloud of soiled napkins clogging the trap, it floated. A bloody sac, clotted expelled human tissue of what would have been January's child. I held my breath and clenched my teeth as I reached down into the toilet bowl and scooped the bloody mass, quickly wrapping it in a discarded paper towel before shoving it into the Crown Royal bag. I carried the bag back to January and placed it in her hand. I used her pashmina to wipe her legs clean.

"I finally unbolted the bathroom door. Jack stood on the other side surrounded by half a dozen angry women.

"'Not my fault you all have weak bladders,' I said, shoving my way through with January's arm over my shoulders.

"I walked her straight out the back door. Then I found a place near the tracks where the earth was soft and pulled Jack's pocket knife from my garter, using it to dig a small hole. We placed the bag inside the earth and covered it back up with some rocks. I took January home and stayed with her until she eventually cried herself to sleep.

"Driving home, I stopped at a local drug store. I made my way to the cleaning supply aisle and purchased a large gallon of bleach. The cashier eyed me, terrified, as I reached out with dried blood under my nails but said nothing as I paid with a fistful of crinkled dollar bills and quickly shuffled out.

"Once at home I filled the tub with steaming hot water and climbed in, still dressed, clutching the bottle of bleach to my chest. Oddly, the tears didn't start falling until I began to unscrew the lid. My hands smelled sour, and the dried secretion left behind reminded me that the dismissed membrane I'd touched was someone's unborn child, another dream gone. I dumped the entire bottle of Clorox in the water and just sat there letting it sting as it cleansed the color right out of the fabric of my clothing. My eyes burned so badly. I let it burn, sitting there, crying for January.

"Time went on, and January eventually returned to her normal self. Whenever I saw her staring off for too long, I'd go over and quickly get her mind off it all. But some nights, I'd pull up to the club and see her shadow in my headlights standing over the very spot where we'd buried him, the child who never got a name. She'd see me watching her, but we never spoke about it again. Never. The other girls never knew of that misfortune. Jack noticed after a while that January's tummy wasn't getting any bigger, but he never said a thing. I think it was his way of being supportive, sparing her an explanation."

Chapter 10

"Every job is demanding in its own way. Some days you need a lot more patience to keep your anger from causing you legal problems. It's called work for a reason—blood, sweat, and tears all shed for the sake of livelihood. Sometimes they get shed at once. Being an entertainer, however, remains the most physically draining occupation I've ever had. I can't tell you how many nights I went home limping on swollen feet from those ridiculously high pumps we were forced to prance around in every night, but beauty is pain. My hands grew calluses that would eventually split and bleed from pulling my body weight up the pole. Most nights after showering I was too tired to even count my tips. Most working people watch the clock. We watched the sky from a small dressing room window. Once it was up, it was time to go.

"'See you all tomorrow!' I said, reaching for my seatbelt early one Sunday morning. Harris turned the corner to enter the building as I cranked my car. Soon as the engine roared and I turned on the heat, I felt two hands wrap around me from the backseat.

"'Gotcha! Time to die, princess!'

"I screamed bloody murder.

"'Relax! Relax! It's just me,' Valentine said, laughing.

"'What the hell is wrong with you! You almost gave me a heart attack!'

"'Calm down, soap opera actress; it was just a joke. Lighten up. You're supposed to laugh. Do you remember what that feels like? Laughter, fun? Or have you become a complete prude altogether? You may as well adopt a cat and start antiquing,' she said, climbing from the backseat to the front.

"'Get your feet off my seat! You're getting mud everywhere! What the hell are you doing in my car, and how did you get in? It was locked.'

"'We used to be best friends, remember? I know you keep a spare taped under the license plate. I'm the one who told you to hide it there after that time we got locked out at the mall, remember? I wanted to bust the window out, you wanted to call pop-a-lock. We went back and forth for an hour.'

"'That doesn't give you the right to use it and let yourself in like you own it.'

"'Right, 'cause you don't associate yourself with me anymore. Halo's your new best bud now, huh? You guys sure are thick as thieves lately. What's next, matching tattoos?'

"I ignored that comment altogether, since it was a petty attempt to ignite trifling tension. 'Look, I'm exhausted. I don't have time for this. What do you want, Valentine?'

"'Well, I'm starving. I thought we could go get some waffles and bacon at the diner, just me and you. I know you hate coffee unless it has ice in it, so I'll sneak my flask in and spike the orange juice instead, just like old times.'

"'No, not interested. Some other time,' I answered dryly.

"'Come on. I know you're hungry. You put in just as many hours as me tonight. We could switch it up if you want, get a short stack of pancakes to share, add some blueberries or pecans. Do you think there's a peach pancake out there in the world? I bet that would taste good …'

"'I said no! What part of *no* don't you understand?'

"'How many times do I have to apologize before you believe me when I say that I never meant for stuff to go down the way it did at the High-Rise?'

"'Valentine, you think saying you're sorry is going to fix it? It's over and done. There's nothing you can do about it now. It's not fixable. I just wanna forget about it and move on with my life.'

"'But why do you have to forget about me too?'

"'I really should get home. I have a day job.'

"'Well, could you give me a ride home at least?'

"'Not if you have drugs on you.'

"'I don't, I promise.'

"'Then you won't mind if I check your jacket pocket? Maybe underneath your hat? See if you're stashing anything in your sock?'

"Valentine looked out the window with a heavy sigh.

"'That's what I thought. Get out of my car. You can call a cab or walk. I don't care if you gotta get home on a skateboard just as long as you get out of this car right now.'

"Valentine said nothing as she got out and slammed the door. I drove away without looking back."

Chapter 11

"Trauma. So much of it, in so many different forms. All those bad things I witnessed in the dark … I waited for them to come to light, but in the meantime the suppressed realities began to manifest themselves in other ways. The bigger the secret, the bigger the hole you have to dig, and all that means is that you're gonna need a much bigger shovel because you're going to need more dirt. An unresolved aching will never rest in peace. I learned that in my time employed at the club. Bury it with dirt, drown it in booze, postpone the pressures of society with drugs, or numb it with emotionless demeaning sex, but none of the above will give you lasting peace.

"I don't remember when the nightmares started, but they came strong. The copious perspiration, the tossing and turning, they always came about an hour into sleep like clockwork, the product of guilt, no doubt. Things like that tend to happen when you know you ain't living right."

"Nightmares?"

"Nightmares? As in multiple? No. Just the one. One nightmare recurring over and over again, every night. It was like my brain was stuck on repeat or something."

"So you continuously suffered the same night terror?"

"Yes."

"Tell me about it."

"I dreamed about myself dancing nearly nude beneath the burning heat of the colorful lights. The crowd roared and cheered, goading me on as my hips swayed, winding like a serpent, and I charmed. My batting lashes deceived dummies by the dozen. *Mafia! Mafia! Mafia!* they called, breaking apart the syllables in chant the way a pep squad would at a home game. They begged for more, and I was ready to give more and more. I loved it; it's true. All eyes were locked on me and my shameless beauty. I ran my hands down my body so they could pretend my hands were theirs and my flesh was there for beholding, appreciation. I was on fire, burning from the inside, and their obsession was sweet kerosene that I gladly devoured to better quench my thirst for attention. I wanted it, their stare. I needed it. I had to have it. It was the closest thing to love I could allow myself to feel and I couldn't stop. But then ..."

"What happened?"

"The music stops in the nightmare. The lights start to dim on my set. The crowd disperses. They all turn to leave, walking away from the chairs surrounding the stage. 'No! Don't go!' I beg. 'Look at me! I'm beautiful! Don't go! Come back! Please! Want me! Need me! Love me!' As the nightmare ends, I'm all alone on the stage, clinging to my private parts. The club empties, and I just sit there alone, crying, until the lights are all the way gone and the whole place is completely engulfed in darkness."

Chapter 12

"Do you believe in divine intervention, Ms. Foxx?"

"Divine intervention? Yes, of course. Most religious people do."

"I believe in it too. I believe that sometimes we need a higher power to step in, reroute us so that we are in a specific place at a specific time to either make something happen or stop something from happening. Maybe we're just there to present a chance, give someone a chance to make the right choice. See if they're ready for the life they've been praying for.

"It was an ordinary night, at first. I stopped at the Quickie convenience store on the corner, about a mile from the club, for an energy drink. I bantered with the clerk like always before walking back out to fill my gas tank. I was leaning against the trunk chewing licorice when an aluminum can—rolling across the asphalt parking lot with the assistance of the wind—startled me. I walked over and picked up, starting for the dumpster, pretending to dribble it between my legs. 'She shoots, but will it count?' I joked in my best sportscaster voice. I'd stopped a few feet away and tossed it like a basketball. 'All net! The crowd goes wild!'

"I was just about to walk away when I noticed movement near the base of the big trash receptacle behind the station. 'Who's there?' I asked, my hand over my suddenly racing heart. I was afraid at first but then figured it was just a homeless person in need of help.

"'Oh my goodness,' I said, rushing over, removing my jacket and wrapping it around the stranger's shoulders. At second glance I realized it was a familiar face. 'Olive …'

"She looked me right in the face. She was there in the flesh but strangely absent in the eyes. Her cheek was bruised to a blue shade. Her hair was sticky with rotted garbage residue.

"She staggered to her feet, and I grabbed her arm tight to help steady her, but she screamed the minute I touched it. 'My arm! It hurts!'

"'Here, let me see.' I carefully maneuvered her sleeve for a better look. It was limp and nearly purple. 'It might be fractured. What happened to you?'

"'Tosh got mad at me,' Olive whispered.

"'That guy Tosh from the club did this to you?'

"'It's really my fault,' Olive mumbled feebly. 'I didn't make enough money last night. Not even enough to pay for our hotel room. He said I didn't make enough to sleep under a roof. We started arguing and he made me get out of the truck and stay here on the card board. He said it would build character, teach me to appreciate all he provides for me, but he said he's coming back and I'd get another chance to earn a warm bed to sleep in tonight, a floor beneath my feet instead of concrete. I didn't apply myself. I should've tried harder, made myself look better, made them want me more.'

"'What? No, sweetie, you didn't do anything wrong.'

"'I did. I was sluggish, but I'll do better tonight. I'll do better, Mafia—he'll see.' Her eyes were child-like, as if begging for me to promise her that tonight would be better.

"'You can't go to work like this. You're hurt. Come, let me get you to a doctor.'

"'No, I can't go. I'm waiting for Tosh.'

"'Look at you! You can barely stand. Have you even eaten?'

"'I ate four days ago.'

"'Olive, listen to yourself! Can't you see what you've been reduced to? It's servitude! Please, let me get you to someone who can help, a place where you can detox. My home can be your home. We can find your family back in Tennessee. They must be worried sick.'

"She was weepy and resistant, but I eventually convinced her to walk toward my car. We were almost there when Tosh's truck pulled up, blocking our path.

"'Olive! Girl, where do you think you're going?' he yelled.

"I could almost feel her body temperature drop. 'Nowhere. I wasn't going anywhere, we were just—'

"'Just what?' he barked.

"I spoke up, as if to protect Olive. 'She's coming with me. She's not going anywhere with you! I'm taking her to get the help she needs. The best thing for you to do is just get out of here.'

"'And if I don't, Mafia? What you gonna do, snitch? Call your little lover boy? You think I'm scared of that cop-boyfriend of yours?"

"'I don't need him to deal with you. You don't scare me, not even a little bit. In fact, I'm way scarier than you. Maybe you haven't heard? Men like you disgust me. Why not bargain with your own body? I could think of at least one hole in you that could use some plugging. But then again, who'd pay for *you*?'

"'You're awfully sassy for a common stripper.'

"'I prefer professional entertainer or pole technician. At least I have a job title. What do you do? Count money? That's what calculators are for, idiot. Hell, almost every smartphone in the world has an app for that now. You know what that means? You're obsolete. You're literally good for nothing.'

"'Smart girl. You're right, I am good with numbers. I'm good with addresses too. That officer you're dating, does he still live over on Sonesta Boulevard? Second house on the left, am I right? And you, you still renting that townhouse behind the elementary school off Grandberry?'

"I stood very still. Neither Tosh nor I blinked.

"'There's an app to help navigate me right to those places if I wanted to go there, got one on almost every smartphone in the world now, just like those nifty calculators.'

"I didn't wanna be scared, but I was just a little.

"'Olive I'm going to make this real simple for you. You rolling with me or you staying here with her? Pick one. Before you answer, know that once I retire you, you're done for good. Ain't nobody else gonna market you, too many miles.' He pointed at me. 'She has an education to fall back on, that's why she's so quick to talk back. What do you have?'

"I looked over at Olive, but she refused to look me in the face. Instead, she pulled away and removed my jacket, handed it back to me. 'He's the only family who cares,' she muttered.

"I watched her wobble all the way to his truck. A smirk stretched across his face as they drove away.

"I stood there for a minute in the cold. Finally, I walked back over to the car. The gas pump was finished filling my tank, but I didn't remove the nozzle right away. I just sat shivering in my car without the heat on. I didn't go in to work that night. I couldn't bear to see Olive weakly limping around the club, begging for money just to avoid another beating. The very thought of it made me want to cry because I'd learned to love those girls. Every night I prayed that they loved me back. Love will grow between those you suffer with.

"All the nights following were different. Olive would see me, and without speaking a word, my eyes said to her, *I'm sorry I didn't fight harder to protect you.* Without speaking, her eyes replied, *Thank you for caring enough to try. No one else ever did.*"

Chapter 13

"Sex and lovemaking are two very different things, Diana. Did you know that? Fools try to convince themselves that one can be the other, but that can never be. Many women claim to have swapped souls with men. In reality, all they did was invite an undeserving male inside of them to relieve lustful pressure, trying to reach the heart using less powerful body parts. Oh yes, they couldn't be more different. One is only the physical act of desire. It can be performed well, just like dancing a stage set. But the real lovemaking can never be an act because it's not a performance. It's not acting. It's a moment inside an emotion wrapped in a revelation. It either is, or it isn't, love. Accept no imitations, cheat yourself not, for goodness sake.

"'It's raining outside.' I'd said it to him as soon as the ringing on the line ceased, without allowing him to say hello in return.

"'Raining—yes, I noticed. It's coming down pretty hard,' Princeton said.

"'Weather app on my phone says it's going to be like this all night long. Nasty weather, typically bad for business. Only seasoned bar patrons, professional drinkers, and spectators who never tip come in. The occasional construction worker getting rained out of a day's work, maybe. Still not worth going in. I was thinking about taking the night off, admire the storm. I was thinking maybe we could admire it together.'

"'Together?' I could sense the anticipation in Princeton's voice, though he tried to hide it behind a masculine façade. 'Really? Yeah, that would be great.'

"'Good, because I'm already at your door,' I confessed.

"I hung up and knocked. Princeton answered with the phone still to his cheek.

"'Hey,' he said, stunned by my unexpected visit.

"'Hey yourself,' I replied from beneath my umbrella.

"He smiled and pulled me inside with an embrace. 'A rainbow before rain's end? How special,' he said, comparing my smile to a spectrum in the sky, which made me blush.

"Princeton took my coat, and I strolled around his apartment, admiring the unique decor. 'These paintings—did you do all of them yourself?'

"'Yes.'

"'They're absolutely phenomenal,' I said, running my fingertips over the many canvases.

"'They're okay, It's mostly just a hobby. It keeps my head clear when I'm not busy protecting and serving.'

"'No, they're amazing, truly. Honestly.'

"'Not exactly museum-worthy ...'

"'Didn't your mother ever teach you how to gracefully accept a compliment, Officer Cambridge? It's awfully rude not saying thank you,' I said with a playful smirk.

"'You're right. Thank you,' he replied with a handsome sneer.

"'You're most welcome, pig.'

"'I stopped near an easel with unfinished peach and umber hue brushstrokes. The pastels seemed to leap right off the parchment. 'What do you call this one?'

"'It's currently an untitled piece. I was thinking about calling it "Reese."'

"'Reese?'

"'Yes. You see, the woman in this painting is bound, wrapped in her own hair, but if you look closely you'll see that it isn't just a long braid, it's a chain. It binds her, her very own beauty. And even though she's captive, she's free in her heart to love if she chooses. However, her focus remains on the sky, not on what holds her back, denying its power though it may bring pain. Looking to the hills ...'

'From which cometh her help ...' I finished.

"'Yes, that's how the scripture goes, something like that. I think that's a perfect title for this piece. It's a special piece, so it's namesake should be just as special.'

"'How philosophical, how smooth.'

"Princeton eyed me curiously, tilting his head to the side as if to figure me out. 'How often do you feel beautiful?'

"'What a peculiar question.'

"'Peculiar maybe, but I'd still like an answer. Tell me, how often do you feel pretty?'

"'Pretty? Me? Never. Not even when I'm dancing on stage.'

"'So no one's ever told you that you're breathtaking?'

"'Oh yes, many times.'

"'You don't believe them?'

"'No. You see, everyone sells candy nowadays—sweetly addictive but potentially flattering, rotten little lies. Every word that comes out of a customer's mouth is to be considered bait. My mind just works like that. Maybe I think too much. I honestly feel ugly. I always have. I've never confessed that to anyone. Even when you say it, that I'm pretty, I feel nothing.'

"'Okay, so you think too much. Enough about your busy mind; what about your heart?'

"'What about it?'

"'When I say things to you like I care for you. I need you. I think you're beautiful. What do you feel in your heart?'

"Thunder cracked outside and I flinched.

"'Are you afraid?' Princeton asked.

"'Of what?' I asked defensively.

"'Of the storm. What else?' he asked, moving closer.

"'No, not of that,' I answered, countering his approach with a few tentative steps of my own.

"'Then of what?' He slowly unbuttoned his shirt. 'Of me?'

"'Maybe. Haven't decided yet.'

"'Elaborate, please.'

"'It's the aftermath of us that I fear. I've been warned about it.'

"'Aftermath?' he asked, stroking my cheek.

"'Yeah. When you decide to run away. They always go away, the people you trust.'

"'Not all of them.'

"'Yes. All of them. I'm not exaggerating just to be dramatic. I mean *all*, in every sense of the word. There's a crossroads where you choose to listen to your heart and ignore all the bells in your head, the ones that try to remind you of the last time and the time before that. Most times the hopeless romantics like me take the route that should lead us straight to love.

"But then it all falls apart; it always does. Wedding dresses turn into waiting dresses, 'cause after a while you're just waiting for them to fall in love with you again. Wondering if it's even possible at all. There will be no more hopeful thoughts or forget-me-nots. The safe place in the arms of the safe person, it turns into winter. And then you'll force me to learn to live without you. One day you'll push me away, and I'll beg you to stay. One day the little things you once loved about me will repulse you like sewer filth festering beneath the city. You'll hate touching me. You won't look at me. You won't stay. I'll be on my own all over again. Yes, I'm terrified, I'll admit. What if you hurt me?'

"'I wouldn't.'

"'You could.'

"'But I never will.'

"'And if you do? What will become of me then? The vultures, the ones who hurt me before, they've left so little of me. Would I survive another heartbreak? What if you do? What if you hurt me?'

"'Then I'd be denying myself. I'd be denying who I am.'

"'And who's that?'

"'I'm the man who was made for you. My heart isn't on my sleeve, Reese, it's in my chest. Do you think I'm so full of pride that I can't tell you how I feel? Do you think I'll feel weak? I have no riches, very little to offer, perhaps a gentle shoulder when your regrets resurrect and swarm. Then we can feel the same thunder deep in one another's quiet storm. I promise I'll always look at you the way I'm looking at you right now. Until selfish eyes no longer grant thee sight. Love either is or it isn't; not even time is a factor. You know if it's the real thing the moment you lock eyes. When you choose to confess it, that's up to you.'

"'Are you saying you love me?'

"'If I was, would you believe me?'

"'What do you think?'

"'I think you *want* to believe me?' Princeton moved even closer.

"'You think you were made for me?' I asked.

"'I'm certain.'

"'But—'

"'But you're afraid, right?'

"'I am ...'

"'But somehow you're here with me, alone. So you're also curious.'

"'Yes, I know,' I whispered, running my hands from his jaw line down his firm chest.

"'Why?'

"'I don't like fear, Officer Cambridge. I could never tolerate it, even as a child. I believe all fears are meant for conquering. It's the only real purpose they serve, when attempting to grow.'

"'So is that why you're here? To conquer me?'

"I felt every exhale on my neck, and his scent began to warm me from the inside out.

"'What are you waiting for?' he asked. 'Let's conquer whatever this is so that we can move on to our next battle, together, and grow together.'

"His kiss was magnetic, in a way that felt destined beyond either of our control. In a way that felt written in the sky by a feather in destiny's grasp. I felt his hands, coarse with calluses, slide so gently from my face down to my ribs. Princeton's lips on my collarbone were the equivalent of a rose petal's silk; soft like a leaf abducted by the wind. *Could he feel me trembling beneath my skin as he undressed me?* -To this very day, I still wonder when I reminisce the very first time we were blessed enough to inherit each other's body.

Up until that moment I never thought I deserved a love like that and to have it graced upon my body and planted in my soul; it reminded me that I'm human. There was an appreciation unleashed from inside us both as we mounted one another's flesh like a king or queen mounting a royal throne. Lust, yes, a few times I'd fallen victim to it, but never had I received such gentleness. For every inch of my skin he provided a specific type of kiss.

"He sang passion in my ear, and I could clearly hear his confession of affection beneath his breath. With every stroke I felt a deepness in his rhythm, one that whispered without words, saying, *This man is making love to you as if he's trying to reach through you and confront the loneliness waiting on the other side, to defeat it one climax at a time because your soul is no longer alone. I am here … with you. And you and I, we've been looking for each other for so long but now I'm here and things are never going to be the same. From now on, when you cry, someone will hold you until the final tear deserts you. And I'll never leave.*

"And there was a white flag in the middle of the war zone, the place where my shame and dismay used to meet and consummate. It wasn't just sex, it was two beautiful people being right where they belonged, tangled up in one another.

"Princeton didn't let go. His grip never loosened for the entire duration of the night. And yes, I was safe. He'll never know this, but I took that night with me; a piece of it remains with me even in this very moment. I saved a little piece of it in my heart, not my memory, my heart, because people tend to forget the things they promise they'll never forget. But you never forget the things you bank in your heart and remind you that God is real.

"I know, without second guessing, there will never be another romance like that one. It killed the bad parts in me and brought life to the dry parts so that they could live again; so *I* could live again. Never will there be another, not in this lifetime or the next. I'm uncertain about a lot of things, but of this I'm sure.

Chapter 14

"I'd learn to love it, the stench of hairspray, scorched synthetic extensions, and cheap perfume. It helped to minimize the smell of nicotine vapor that seemed to linger even when no one was sparking up. I loved the dressing room banter, listening to the girls go back and forth over trending hot news topics. I loved the way we all sang the lyrics to classic throwbacks the DJ would play per request when the club was slow. Eventually, you get into a routine. Get in, get dressed, get on the floor, make the money, and make it home as quickly and safely as possible. Getting comfortable with that routine is dangerous. No one should ever get used to chaos. No matter what, you should never be comfortable in a place like that.

"'Mafia, I need a favor,' Jack said.

"'No,' I replied without taking my concentration off my reflection.

"'You don't even know what I want. At least hear what I want first before you shoot me down.'

"'Okay. Go ahead, pitch.'

"'I've got a new girl coming in. I'm bringing her on board this weekend. I want you to talk to her, give her the rundown on how things work here at Club Malice.'

"'No.'

"'Why not?'

"'No reason, other than I don't feel like it. Why don't you ask someone else?'

"'And risk her picking up whore habits? No, I don't need more of that.'

"'Still no,' I said with a smirk.

"'Tough, you're doing it.'

"'Am not!' I yelled.

"'Are too!' he yelled back, leaving the dressing room.

"'I won't do it!'

"'I owe you one!'

"I smiled and went back to primping. Shortly after, the dressing room door opened again. All the dancers, including myself, turned around, and the room turned dead quiet.

"There she stood, face like a puppy, dressed like a prepubescent nine-year-old.

"'Um … hello. I'm looking for someone name Mafia.'

"Olive elbowed Whisper, and Halo's eyebrows sank, as if thinking, *This girl must be lost.*

"'I was told she'd be back here waiting for me. I think I work here now. I mean, I asked if I'd been hired, and he grunted and made me a drink, so …'

"The room was at a standstill, and everyone stared malevolently at her, as if they were going to eat her alive. I remembered that stare all too well.

"She began to squirm uncomfortably, just like I did when I first met them. 'Should I come back later maybe?'

"'No,' I said, standing. 'Come on back and have a seat right here. I'll take care of you. Would you all stop looking at her like that before you scare her off?'

"Slowly she crept to the chair next to mine and sat. I won't lie—I stared curiously. She seemed far too well kept to be working in a strip club. Maybe a church or finishing school.

"'Are you Mafia?'

"'Yeah, that's me. It's nice to meet you.'

"'Jack says good things about you.'

"'Well, Jack's an expert liar. You can't believe shit he says,' I replied, winking. She laughed, and it seemed to calm her a bit. 'What exactly did he tell you about me?'

"'Jack said you're his favorite. He said you're smart and you couldn't be bought. He also said you're pretty enough to sell a lap dance to a paralyzed man.'

"'Well I'll be damned—all that's true.' We both laughed. 'Jack says you're starting this weekend?'

"'Yeah.'

"'Are you scared?' I asked, blotting my lipstick.

"'Very much.'

"'Why?'

"'I don't know anything about dancing. I don't know anything about seduction. I know nothing about men at all. What if I fall flat on my face? What if I'm not sexy enough? What if I get on stage and no one throws money?'

"I laughed, but not on purpose. The similarities were uncanny. 'You sound like me, the first night I worked a full shift. I was a nervous wreck.'

"'You were?'

"'Oh yes. I'd never worn heels so high. My strut was wobbly, and I tripped a lot. I was probably the most unpoised, inexpert dancer in here, very clumsy in my approach, but I learned. So will you.'

"'But …'

"'But what?'

"'I'm not very pretty.'

"I lowered my mascara and turned to face her. 'One thing I don't ever want you to do is compare yourself to anyone in here. You are you. As long as you're the best version of yourself, you'll do just fine. Look around you. Every woman back here is different. Look at all these shades and sizes, all beautifully made. Some of us have stretch marks. Some of us try to hid the cellulite with one hand and wolf down candy bars with the other. There are at least five wigs in here, and some of these girls have acne that not even the best concealer can hide, so be kind to yourself. You gotta be careful with that kind of inferior thinking. It's that kind of nonsense that will make you believe you need to start changing things about yourself, turn into someone else altogether. Then you'll have cheated the world of your individuality. Tell yourself you're something every single day. Confidence is the sexiest thing you can put on, and you may as well heavily drape yourself in it 'cause you sure ain't gonna be able to wear much of anything when the show starts.'

"'Can you teach me how to be confident?'

"'No, I'm sorry. I can teach you a lot of things, but confidence is not one of them. I can, however, help you look less like a runaway from a farm cult. Come a little closer, let's see what we can do with all this pretty hair you've grown.'

"As I fluffed and curled, we talked about proper and improper club vernacular. While I polished her nails, we went over things that were illegal and the things that would get you fined by the state. By the time I'd applied the first pair of artificial lashes she'd ever worn, we'd cleared every topic from the price of lap dances to floor fees.

"'So why did you decide to dance? You need extra money, or are you trying to teach mommy and daddy a lesson by being a little rebellious?'

"'Money. I need money. A lot of it. And I don't have a lot of time.'

"'How much we talking? Bug money or little money?'

"'Enough to save our house. My daddy owns the pawn shop over on Pitter Street. You know, the historic district where they host the big parade on Labor Day weekend. That store has been in our family for generations. When my mother passed away, I started working to help keep the property taxes on the house and the store in good standing. Daddy is sick now and getting worse. He just can't do as much as he used to. The store isn't doing as well with all these secondhand websites. People can just shop for antiques at home right on their couch. I must do something. I just can't sit and watch him wither away, losing it all. I told him I'd be cleaning overnight for some janitorial company. I didn't want him to be disappointed in me for working here.'

"'Saving the home? Saving the store? You're a good daughter. I know things look hard now, but they'll get better. The money you'll make here is just as green as the money you'd get paid at any other job. There's nothing wrong with doing all you can. I'll be the first to admit I'm not proud to be a dancer, but I'm not ashamed either. I take care of myself. Half the people with opinions have nothing else to offer, no assistance or wisdom. You can't cash in judgment to put food on the table. People had a lot to say about my dancing, even some family members, but I'm willing to bet they'd send my call straight to voice mail if I called for help with rent. Those same folks are quick to call you when they're down and out, begging you for those same tips you earned with your body. Those are the times you have to check your humility. Sure, it would feel good to say no and make them feel lower than they made me feel, but I'll settle for them looking at the ground when it's time for those very same people to defend me in casual conversation. Everything is going to be okay. We'll get the money to save your house and your family's store.'

"'I hope so,' she said sullenly.

"'Are you ready to see your dramatic transformation?'

"'Yes!' she said excitedly. Her face seemed to glow. 'Wow, I look so ... I look so ...'

"'Confident?' I said, completing her sentence.

"'Yes. Thank you so much.'

"'You're most welcome. Just remember these makeup tips, and you'll turn some heads this weekend. The sooner you make the money you need, the sooner you can quit.'

"I'd started putting my cosmetics away when she tapped me on the shoulder, looking around to make sure we were the only ones left in the dressing room. 'Can I ask you something?' She paused for a second. 'People say bad things about places like this. They speak of horrible things, both wicked and unladylike' You seem so sweet and clean. It all seems to ... work for you. Has anything bad ever happened to you since you chose this line of work? Anything that made you regret the day you set foot in here?'

"'No. Never. Not once. I'm a big girl,' I said, looking her dead in the eye as I told her a lie. 'Stop thinking so much; you're never really alone. I keep a bible back here in my locker. We always pray, soon as we're all in attendance. There's no difference between the dangers out there and the dangers in here. It's just that the walls and roof keep it all closer to you is all. Makes it a little harder to avoid. Your eyes and first impression do not deceive you. My conscience, my hands, they're both still clean somehow. Listen. You never have to come back after you make the money you need. You can walk away free and clear. So even *if* there were bad things here, you'll be out way before you become a victim.'

"'Is it that easy?'

"'It can be. That's up to you,' I said, looking away.

"'Alice, that's my name, by the way. You never asked.'

"'I'm sorry, sweetie. It's nothing personal. We usually just wait for the new ones to pick an alias. If Jack don't give you one, it's usually because he doesn't foresee a future for you here, which isn't bad. We don't use real names around here because the real *you* doesn't exist in here. My advice: get a stage name fast, and tell no one who you really are. Never take the same route home, you never know who's waiting to get you alone. Pick only a few to befriend, It's safer that way. Go on, get out of here so I can get changed and get to work. I got money to make. You're holding me up with all this personal stuff. I'll see you this weekend.'

"After she was gone, I looked around at all the lockers and mirrors, fighting the burning sensation in the corners of my eyes. I sat down in the middle of the dressing room and thought about Alice's question: 'Has anything bad ever happened to you since you chose this line of work?' I'd said no, but then I thought about the high rise. And then I began to cry.

"Remember Me Red was the name of the clever shade of polish I'd purchased the day before. You'd be surprised how many men like feet. They're sick and twisted freaks of nature, wanting to massage and lotion them. Sometimes they'd just walk right up to the stage and ask to see your toes like they had no shame at all. They'd rather your feet be pretty than your face, which I personally find insulting, but the girls with princess feet made a lot of cash. So naturally I spent that day off at home, preening everything below the ankle. I had no original plans for the night other than tending to my stage bruises and pole burn. I shouldn't have answered the phone that night. I think about that a lot. What if I'd sent that call to voice mail? Would things have turned out the same?

"'Hey, bookworm! What are you doing?' Valentine had a way of being delightfully bad-mannered and comical at the same time.

"'Nothing much really. Just finished soaking in mint water. Pretty sure I'm going to have to invest in those leg warmers you suggested if I'm ever going to wear shorts again. My right shin is banged up. Finally giving myself a pedicure. I'm embarrassed by the amount of attention my feet need. I wish we could dance in sneakers.'

"'That sounds so boring. I literally just yawned.'

"'Very funny. I was just about to text you to see if you wanted to come over for a girls' night. Maybe watch a scary movie. I got some kettle corn in the kitchen, so say the word and I'll pop it. I got the pizza place on speed dial.'

"'I got a better idea. Why don't you come with me to a party I'm hosting.'

"'A party?'

"'Yeah, just a small get-together with some super chill friends; nothing too big. We can have a few drinks on their dime.'

"'A party? It's kind of late.'

"'It's barely after midnight, Grandma. Splash some water on your face and hop to it; there's a lot of money to be made.'

"'Money?'

"'Yeah, a bunch. These jerks are so filthy rich that they leave the tip line blank when they eat out. They want dancers, just to serve drinks and parade around in swimsuits. Easiest money you ever gonna make, way easier than suffering eight to nine hours working the floor at the club. Please come; I don't wanna go alone. It'll be fun; you'll see. I got your back. You trust me, right?'

"'Of course.'

"'Then get up and get dressed! I'm on my way there now. I'll meet you there. I'm texting you the address now, okay? Bye!'

"Valentine hung up before I even had a chance to accept, but I got up and dressed. Then I stuffed my work bag with a few of my favorite undergarments to impress.

"I'll never forget that address: 4112 Grand Chenier Avenue. It was on the fancier side of town where people performed street art even after dark and smiled even when they didn't get tipped. The old ladies who ride the bus don't clutch their purses tight because they don't fear thieves. The people on the sidewalks say good morning or good evening; it's only weird if you don't say it back.

"I strolled into the High-Rise Grand Hotel with my tote hanging on my shoulder like a bag lady. The atrium was weirdly quiet, so quiet I could hear every stroke of the custodian's mop in the lobby, even his fatigued, offbeat panting. I approached the desk clerk, double-checking Valentine's last message before asking for directions to the elevator.

"'What room are you looking for?'

"'I think it's the ambassador suite, room 5056.'

"'You'll wanna take the elevator down the hall up to the fourth floor and then take the stairs up. Less traffic.'

"'Okay, thank you.'

"'Have fun …' It was odd, the shifty, shady facial expression he'd made when he'd said it, but I boarded the elevator anyway.

"After a few taps the suite door finally opened, releasing the stench of questionable herb smoke into the hallway. I expected Valentine to answer, but instead I found myself standing face-to-face with a plain suit I'd never seen before. 'Well hi there, you must be the new hot product.'

"'Excuse me'? I asked, appalled and confused.

"'Was that a little too forward? My apologies. I've probably had one too many glasses of wine. Here, let me shake your hand. My name is … well, never mind that. I'm sure you're going to give me some generic code name, so I guess you can call me … Mr. S. Come on in. Can I get you a drink, or any other form of comfort? We've got things you can smoke. We've got things you can inject and chew. We've got things you can sniff. Hell, it's safe to say we've got a little bit of everything in here to party. What are you into? Don't be ashamed, you beautiful devil, we all have our delightful vices. Comfort is bliss. And we all deserve bliss.'

"'Can you just tell me where I can find my friend?'

"'Your friend? Well, we're all friends here.'

"'No we're not. I meant my real friend, the one who invited me here to help out—Valentine.'

"'Why don't you get to know me first and then I'll take you straight to her? That's a promise.'

"'Mr. Sims, you dog! Get off her leg before she spooks. She's never served before,' Valentine yelled from the back of the suite. 'I'm sorry, babe. He's just an old hound. Can't you tell? Don't pay him any mind. Come with me; I'll get you something cold and fruity to sip and then you can get changed.'

"'I've never seen so many designer watches in my life,' I said to Valentine once we were alone. 'Who are these rich jerks?'

"'Longtime friends.'

"'Friends? Funny how I never met them before, or seen them in the club. Are they from out of town?'

"Valentine laughed and her glazed eyes betrayed her, revealing her obvious high. 'Out of town? More like from another planet. Weirdos, they are. Beasts, these men.'

"She set her drink down and proceed to dig through my bag. 'You brought the turquoise bra set. That's good! That's so good! I love you in this; put it on! You're going to look so pretty! They're going to go crazy like gorillas pounding their own chests! Here, let me help you put it on,' she said, tearing at my hoodie.

"'I can do it, Valentine,' I said, grabbing her wrists.

"'I just wanna help,' she said, playing in my hair.

"'Valentine! Stop. I can dress myself. Been doing it since I was five. I think I can manage,' I said, trying to figure out why she was suddenly so anxious.

"'You're right. I'm sorry. I'm just so happy you're here is all. You know how I love spending time with you. Go ahead, get dressed, take your time,' she said, backing off. 'They pay you after the party. Don't worry, they're good for it. Everything's straight cash on the table.'

"'Okay. Well, where's my tray?'

"'Tray?'

"'Yeah, it's kind of hard to serve drinks with no tray.'

"'Oh right, about that. There's been a little change of plans.'

"'What kind of change?'

"'They don't need us to carry no tray. You'll be serving, but not drinks.'

"'I don't understand. Are we dancing? I didn't see a pole or nothing.'

"'Not exactly.'

"'Valentine! Let's go! It's time to party!' a voice on the other side of the door said.

"'What does he mean?' I asked Valentine, who'd rushed to the mirror, touching up her lip gloss.

"'Look. I need you right now, okay, sweetie? Be a big girl for me. I need you to stop asking so many questions. They don't pay us to talk and they hate questions. *Yes* is the only word they care to hear. No complaining either. They get enough of that at home with their overbearing wives. Now I won't let anything bad happen to you. Never. I know these guys, they're practically harmless. Been dealing with them for years, but they get bored with the same old thing, you know? When I told them I had a new face and firm new body, way less touched than mine, they got real excited and the numbers just went up and up.'

73

"'Valentine, what's going on?'

"'They got the good stuff, Mafia. Not that half percent product I'm used to. They got the money, company accounts with no limit. What more could a girl ask for? Drugs and money, it's like a dream come true. Consider all the things I've done for you. I taught you everything you know. You couldn't even spin on the pole without falling on your ass. I need you to do this for me.'

"'Do what?'

"'They just wanna touch you a little bit. That's all, nothing rough or weird.'

"'Have you lost your mind?' I asked, turning two shades more pale.

"'Please don't get all prissy on me. It's not like you're a virgin. Don't make me look bad. I told them you were down.'

"'Well then get your ass back out there and tell them you lied! That there was a big misunderstanding! I'm not down with whatever you're talking about! I'm not cool with any of this! How dare you trick me into coming down here!'

"'Is it okay if we join you guys,' asked the suit, strolling in with all his colleagues behind him, all eight of them disrobing in unison.

"'Of course you can,' Valentine said. 'Suck it up, okay?'" she muttered, fluffing my hair. 'Who taught you to dance? Who taught you to own the crowd? Who made you? Me. I did that. Now Just do what they say. Do it right, and they'll ask us to keep coming back. We'll be like business partners … best friend business partners. Doesn't that sound good?'

"I watched Valentine climb on the king-sized pillow-top mattress. All the men followed without speaking. My stomach began to turn as I watched them all start to caress one another, exchanging intimate rubs.

"'Watch for a while. Feel free to join in anytime,' the suit said.

"I was frozen. I wanted to scream for help, but it was like I'd momentarily lost my voice. I eventually felt my blood flowing again. I had to run. There was no way in hell I was letting any of them touch me. I slowly backed out of the room, grabbing my hoodie off the chair.

"'Where are you going?' Valentine asked from underneath the pile of naked men. 'Mafia, wait, come back!' she yelled as I darted for the door.

"I escaped the suite, running as fast as I could down the stairs, and when the elevator door opened I ran some more, straight past the check-in desk and down the city street until I reached the bus. I hysterically banged on the glass doors, paying no attention the "out of service" light overhead.

"The driver stuffed his sandwich back in his lunch box and opened the doors. 'Don't you go breaking my glass! Don't you see the sign? This bus ain't running right now. I'm on break.'

"'Please, I need to go home! I … there was a party … I can't go back. Please. My phone, it's in my bag. My wallet's back there. I don't have any money!'

"He looked down at my freshly polished toenails, bare feet on the pavement. I clutched the front of my hoodie, trying to hide my half-naked body. 'You in some kind of trouble?'

"'Yes. No. I mean … I'm not sure.' I tried to explain. 'I need to go home. Please! I want to be in my room! In my own bed! With no one else!'

"'Sweetheart, it's all right. Calm down. Just get on.'

"The driver dropped me off as far as the city line. I was too scared to return to my apartment, thinking they'd come for me to collect whatever Valentine had promised them, so I walked for miles until I reached my mom's house in the country.

"When I got there I retrieved to spare key from under the mat. I ran inside and locked the door. I stayed in a closet until morning.

My mother eventually found me inside, face red and scared. "'Are you hurt?' she asked.

"'No, ma'am.'

"'What happened?'

"'I saw the world, Momma.'

"'It's about time. We don't live in a pay-it-forward kind of world. Most people you meet are takers. Don't think you're not a target just because you don't have much. Hell, they'll find a way to heist anything, whether it's a dollar or hope. It doesn't have to fit in a knapsack for somebody to run off with all your things. Come on out when you're ready. I want you to tell me all about it, you hear me?'

"'Yes, ma'am.' Eventually, I climbed out. I showered the tar from the bottom of my feet, noticing that they weren't pretty anymore, and cried ferociously as I explained to my mother that I took my clothes off for money. I told her about Valentine and what had happened.

"'Just thank the Lord you didn't get hurt. That situation could have played out a hundred different horrible ways. Sometimes the monsters are standing right next to you and you never even notice. Then you start to question, "Why didn't I see it before?" Then you ask yourself, "Did I not see it because I'm becoming what they are? Do they sit right beside me because they feel as if they're among friends?"'

"Diana, do you think we could take a break?" Reese asked, eyes watering.

"Of course."

As soon as Reese was clear from view, chatter began to roar. "We are still on set, people! I won't allow gossip while you're all on my time! Do it online like real scoundrels," Diana snapped.

Intern Tommy entered the interview room and leaned in. "Ms. Diana, Mr. Pete wants to see you again."

Chapter 15

Pete sat at his desk cracking pistachios, spitting shell casings on the floor. "Ms. Foxx, come in. Close the door."

"You asked to speak with me again?"

"Yeah, I did."

"Well, I'm in the middle of the interview, so—"

"Yes, the interview. I've been watching from back here."

"What do you think so far?"

"So far so good … but that's just it. It's only good. It could be better. It should be a lot better. In fact, it *should* be great."

"How so?"

Pete spit more shells onto the desktop and leaned in. "The questions—when do you plan to get to the juicy questions? That's what the viewers want to see."

"Juicy? That's not exactly a word that comes to mind when discussing a national tragedy."

"Tragedy? Oh grow up! Don't be so soft! This is mainstream media, not some sad documentary. You have to keep the people intrigued! Not put them to sleep!"

"Not a tragedy?" she asked incredulously.

"No! No!" Pete yelled, slamming the pack of pistachios on the desk. "This is about her and her lifestyle!"

"I'm not sure what you want me to do!"

"I want you to nail her to the wall! Finish her! There are questions that the good people of this town need answers to. How much does a lap tramp make a night? Can all dancers pick up a dollar bill using only their ass, no hands? Do any men of power party there? Who's the club's main drug proprietor? Are the owners into anything shady? Is a dollar still an acceptable tip amount? How many times a night are they required to change their thongs?"

"Mr. Pete, I can't ask her things like that. She's not a bad person. Reese is not a criminal, and she's not on trial here. She hasn't done anything wrong. She's not an informant or a narc. She's a victim! She's a survivor!"

"A hero?" Pete asked sarcastically.

"Yes! Yes she is! She's an icon—maybe not as innocent or consecrated as your average comic book action figure, but yes! She made it out! Reese outlived the lifestyle. She returned from the fire untouched. My sources confirm, she has no criminal record. She's a pillar of health. She's a productive member of society with a bright future. In fact, she's in better condition now than when she went in. She's smarter, stronger."

"*She's a pole cat!* That's what she is." Pete was nearly red in the face. "I know all about her background. I don't care about her stats or the facts. People don't give a damn about good girls in bad places. They want to hear about the bad girls in bad places doing bad things. These clubs are septic tanks, full of filth. Surely a woman with your history can relate."

"Me? Relate? I'm sorry—what is that supposed to mean?"

Pete stood and fingered through the file cabinet. "Foxx, you're an investigative journalist. Answer this for me: When did Club Malice first open for business?"

"Three years ago."

"That's correct. Three years before that, there was a very lucrative gentlemen's club over on the Southside that went down just like Club Malice, violently and suspiciously. It was a really rowdy place, that club. Do you know the place I'm talking about?" Pete asked.

"Yes," she answered, looking away, humiliated.

"You were employed there for some time. As an entertainer?" he asked, making air quotes around the word *entertainer*, adding insult to injury.

"How dare you."

"Relax, don't get all bent outta shape. I knew long before I hired you. I won't lie, your being so easy on the eyes had a lot to do with my calling you in for a second interview, but the main reason I brought

78

you on board was that fire in your belly, a real hungry drive. A trait I'm guessing you mastered at your previous place of employment. You know, hustling for tips and all. Don't look so offended; you've done well for yourself. You appear very sanitary for an ex-dancer. If I hadn't noticed the big gap in your resume, I wouldn't have even run a background check on you."

"Here I was thinking you genuinely respected me all this time."

"Oh, I respect you plenty, enough to give you first chair and keep this permanent record from the human resources committee. Aside from Kirk the cameraman, no one else knows but you and me."

"Kirk knows!"

"Yes, but *I* didn't tell him. He just happened to be a fan of yours back when you worked the pole. He's a strip club groupie and a drunk, but he knows his way around set equipment. Don't worry. I remind him of our sexual harassment clause every time I see him staring at you longer than a minute when you're off camera."

"I thought today was a dream come true. I thought today would be one of the greatest days of my life," Diana said, suddenly feeling lightheaded.

"No, my dear. I'm afraid it's just another nightmare. A nightmare called life. The only beauty in it all is the birth of a thriving career if you have the guts to dig deep. The news is not a fairy tale for soft people, it's real social concerns woven together by opposing standpoints, accusations, and public interest. Now go do your job or I'll find an anchor who's not afraid to get dirty. I won't hand my station over to a weakling. I need someone to stand up, break the rules, and take charge. Take the high road if you want, but you might not have a job afterward. Now get in there and finish the interview."

Chapter 16

"Have you ever been held, Diana?"

"Yes."

"Well, I'm sure you have at some point. It's not uncommon for the number of lovers to accumulate over the years—we've all had one or two. Some people have had a few that actually meant something to them. But have you ever been held to the point where you start to trust against your better efforts to avoid developing feelings?"

Diana said nothing. Instead, her face tightened and the camera crew looked away.

"Well, then I feel sorry for you. I've been held to that point. I've been loved like that.

"Mornings with Princeton were God's way of repaying me for all the horrors from the nights before. Princeton made things right again. He gave me what I needed to keep going, to keep pushing. Whenever I felt pressure at work, I reminded myself that I was only a sunrise away from seeing him again. I found protection in his arms, that and a lot of other things I never expected to find.

"'If you don't wake up, breakfast will get cold. French toast doesn't taste the same once you microwave it,' Princeton said. 'If you don't get up, I'll be forced to get back in bed with you.'

"'You say that like it's punishment. Sounds more like a good reason to be intentionally disobedient,' I whispered as I sat up, wrapping my arms around his neck. 'Good morning, Officer.'

"'Good morning to you. I cooked for you. I've got an early debriefing, but I wanted to make sure you started the day off right.'

"'How thoughtful. I'll have to think of a way to repay you.'

Princeton set the breakfast plate on a pillow between us and began to feed me.

"'You know, if this is what being spoiled feels like, I must admit I'm a fan,' I said, smirking between chews. I stopped smiling when I noticed Princeton had put the fork down. His face hardened. 'Is something wrong?'

"'Reese, why do you cry in your sleep?'

"I wiped my lips clean and fiddled with the napkin before responding. 'You noticed that?'

"'I notice everything about you.'

"'It's just a bad dream.'

"'Bad dream? Does it have anything to do with the club?' I didn't answer. 'Reese, do you ever think about quitting?'

"'Huh?'

"'Dancing? Do you ever think you about leaving the club, quitting the stripping business? You're not always going to be a stripper, are you?'

"'Stripper? I thought you said you'd never associate me with that word.'

"'Okay then, entertainer. Will you ever quit?'

"I got out of bed and began to dress. 'We talked about this. I'm not comfortable having some man take care of me. I like having my own income. I've been taking care of myself a long time. I'm not gonna be some privileged woman, depending on someone else's paycheck. I wasn't raised like that.'

"'Stop trying to convince me that you're independent. I know you are, I see that strength in you. It's one of the things I love most about you. I'm not asking you to give that up!'

"'Aren't you?'

"'No! I'm asking you to stop taking off your clothes for money! I'm asking you to trust me to provide for us both so that you can focus on your writing!'

"'I can take care of myself!'

"'I know! But you don't belong there. You never did! The moment I saw you running down Grand Chenier, I knew you were better than all the others. This life isn't for you. You were meant to do better, to have better.'

"'What did you just say?'

"Princeton, realizing he'd said too much, lowered his brow.

"'Grand Chenier … I never told you about what happened on Grand Chenier, at the High-Rise.'

"'Reese, I need you to sit down so we can talk.'

"'I don't want to sit down! I want to stand up, and I want you to tell me how the hell you know about the High-Rise!'

"'We were looking for Valentine!'

"'What?'

"'We got a tip from some flea-bitten dancer we busted last year for a DUI. She wanted the judge to go easy on her, so she started talking about drug movement and prostitution. She told stories about how she and another dancer poached customers from the club and went to exclusive parties to perform carnal acts for money, namedropping some prominent people. After we got her a deal in writing, she gave us the mastermind's name. It was Valentine. She was at the center of the entire investigation. We trailed her for a few months, gathered as much as we could on her. We concluded that club management had no idea what she'd been doing, so we focused on her activity outside of the facility. During recon, she was photographed repeatedly, and you were in a lot of those pictures, eating out, shopping with her. We had no intel on who you were. We couldn't find a thing on you, not one offense or arrest. If you hadn't paid with your debit card the last time the two of you had dinner, we would have never known who you were. Lucky for you it's not a crime to befriend a career criminal. When we got wind of another private party going down, we set up in a vacant building across from the High-Rise on Grand Chenier. I thought I was wrong about you when I saw you get off the bus and watched you walk into the High-Rise. In fact, we made a bet, me and the guys, to see if you were going to stay, become what she had become. But you didn't stay. You were so afraid, running down that street. You can't fake that kind of horror, and I wanted so badly to help you, but I couldn't just run after you with a gun and badge.

"'We raided the room soon after, as planned, long enough to catch them in the act. We were unsuccessful. We combed every inch of that suite but couldn't find Valentine anywhere. Desk security showed her slinking out the back a few hours after you bolted. It's strange—she looked directly into the camera on her way down, almost as if she knew we'd be coming for her. The rich pricks got lucky; all we could pin on them were the illegal substances, but it wasn't even enough for a felony charge. I found your bag with your ID before the Calvary could get a hold of it, and I trashed it so they would never know you were there. I didn't want them to think you were involved. My partners helped cover your trail even though they couldn't understand why, claiming they'd only seen one girl head up. For some reason I felt I needed to protect you. The investigation is still open; make no mistake, she's going down. You distancing yourself from her was the best move you ever made, but now it's time for you to walk away from all of it for good. You don't need that place. Yes, the night we finally met, I was undercover, hoping to find a dancer drunk enough to rat somebody else out. But I was secretly hoping I'd run into you and I did.'

"'You were investigating?'

"'Yes, but that's not the reason I got close to you.'

"'You thought I was involved?'

"'I knew you could never be that kind of girl—'

"'You don't know me at all!'

"'Reese, please,' Princeton pleaded.

"'Goodbye, Princeton!' I yelled, storming out.

"'This is one of those things that couples do, right? They fight and then they make up. That's all this is, right? I don't wanna lose you. Tell me this isn't the kind of goodbye that lasts forever.'

"'I don't know yet. Strong chance, though.'"

Chapter 17

"Crying used to be my initial reaction to all things that made me afraid or sad. I used to hate myself for it. It always made me feel so weak in comparison to those who weren't controlled by their emotions. I felt beneath every situation, every heartbreak, every scare. I felt beneath everyone who wished hurt upon me. I used to cry a lot. Emphasis on the past tense of that statement. Sometimes you gotta stop crying and fight back.

"It was the night before the murders. Club Malice was packed, wall to wall. There was little standing room, barely anywhere to sit. I stood at the DJ booth overlooking the crowd, my hips swaying side to side, casually riding the beat like an ocean wave.

"Alice stood next to me, clinging to my side like a child. 'There are so many people!' she yelled, trying to speak over the music. 'I don't think I can do this. I feel sick.'

"'You'll be fine,' I said.

"'But what if—'

"'Look. In here, there is no such thing as tomorrow, yesterday either. Tonight, this very moment, that's all you need to concern yourself about. Be alert and aware and focused.' I grabbed both shoulders and steadied our eye contact. 'Stop worrying! Everything's going to be all right. You're not alone here. There are fourteen other dancers signed in tonight doing the same thing you're doing. Security is deep. You got me and Halo and Whisper. If you get scared or uncomfortable, you come and sit right here in this DJ booth with Saddle. You can see the whole club from up here. Wait for the nearest dancer to pass by and tell her to bring you to wherever I am. Do you understand me?'

"'Okay.'

"'You can trust me. Do you trust me?'

"'Yes,' Alice answered, quivering.

"'Next on the main stage, by request: the one and only Mafia!'

"I gave Saddle a prepared nod and turned my attention back to Alice. 'This will only take a minute. Try to mingle a bit; conversation will help calm you. I won't be far.'

"I rolled my neck around, slow circles clockwise and counterclockwise to loosen the stiffness. Grabbed my legs one at a time, cuffing each ankle, stretching them out. My knuckles popped one at a time, pinky to thumb. Then it was go time. I felt the bass shaking the stage underneath my swift feet. The heat of the multicolored lights felt like the sun, but it was dark, more ways than one, no sun … no stars either. Just the stage, the crowd; no sky, no closer to God.

"In the middle of my set, I noticed a certain gentleman near the stage, watching my every move, tossing obscene amounts of cash on the stage, prompting uproar from the entourage he'd come in with.

"At set's end, Olive approached the edge of the stage. 'The birthday boy wants a champagne room with you.'

"'I could use the money, but I have to pass. I really should stick with Alice tonight. Poor thing's nearly yellow in the face. Bring over one of the other girls and have her introduce herself. They'll bite, I'm sure.'

"'No, he asked for you specifically. He's already paid the bar. He's waiting for you in the back.'

"It was a pet peeve of mine, being summoned as if were an object to be purchased off a shelf with a price tag on my ass, but that was part of the job, feeling objectified and being expected to smile about it. It flattered most girls but not me. I didn't like feeling bought.

"I freshened up and checked into the third champagne room. There he sat, the ecstatic birthday boy, arms stretched across the back of the sofa. His level of intoxication was evident. The degenerate excitement lit on his face as I entered the room induced sudden nausea, but I maintained my composure as best I could.

"'Hello. My name is Mafia. I've been selected to keep you company.'

"'Yes, the dangerous Mafia princess. I know you.'

"'Well, knowing someone and knowing of someone are two completely different things. Kind of like the difference between a friend and an enthusiast, but I'm not here to educate you.'

"'That's right. You're here to entertain me, so dance.' I'd only been in the back for maybe five minutes or so when he began to squirm. I'd seen it before. "'I'm going to take my hat off now,' he said.

"'Suit yourself,' I replied, continuing to dance, focusing on myself in the mirror; anything to keep from looking at him.

"'Can I take off my jacket too?'

"'If you're warm, I can switch on the ceiling fan.'

"'No, that's not necessary. I just wanna get more comfortable, that's all.'

"I turned back and eyed him curiously. 'Your jacket? I suppose that's okay, but I'm afraid that's all you'll be removing—club rules.'

"'So you're saying I can't take these off?' he asked, kicking off his boots.

"'Yes, that's exactly what I'm saying. Sir, I need you to put your shoes back on,' I demanded.

"He laughed at me. 'So I guess my pants are definitely staying on, huh?' he slurred, standing to loosen his belt.

"I sighed heavily. 'Sir, state law requires me to inform you that you are now in clear violation of Club Malice policy. I am forced to end your session. Since the dance has started and you have failed to comply with regulation after being warned, your money is nonrefundable,' I said, turning to the camera, signaling for help, three fingers.

"The customer arose from the couch, nearing me. 'Do not come any closer,' I threatened, signaling for help again.

"'How does this work? You pretend to fight back? Is that part of the show? I'm not into it. I'd prefer you simply submit,' he said grabbing a fistful of my hair, attempting to press his lips on mine.

"'Get your filthy hands off me!' I screamed, pulling and jerking at his paws. 'Harris!'

"My unwillingness to cooperate made the birthday boy angry. 'Shut up! Do you know how much I paid for you? For your *time*? The least you could do is be grateful and give me my happy ending with a smile on your face like a good little stripper,' he mumbled while tearing at my inner thigh.

"'Harris!'

"'I said shut up!' He struck the left side of my face with his knuckles, and the force sent me reeling. His class ring bruised my eye, and I began to bleed from the small cut near my brow.

"The room was suddenly hazy. I looked up at him as he continued to take off his clothes, and I knew what I had to do. I felt the rage again. It was the same familiar rage I felt and loved that day I followed Jack into the club smelling of gasoline. Flashbacks of what happened before I found myself crying in the parking lot began to swarm. I remembered my ex telling me I was nothing, abusing me almost every day. Dragging me from a place he once begged me to call home, telling me I would never amount to anything and that I was trash.

"'Books? You wanna write books? That's your dream, to be on a best seller list one day? That's the stupidest thing I ever heard. Who the hell wants to read something you wrote? You come from nothing … you'll always be nothing!'

"He'd taken my poems and shredded them right in front of me. Spit on the shreds and then spit on me. I snapped that day. Something inside me exploded and I decided I wasn't going to take it anymore. I wanted to take all his beautiful things away from him; maybe then he would feel as hopeless and ugly as he had made me feel. I wanted it all to burn. I remember the flames growing as I continued to douse the fuel, and as the fire consumed, I felt a cleansing as if it purified me. I drove away crying that day. But it was the last time I'd ever cried over a man. It was the last time I'd let words hurt me. That's when I became her, Mafia. I didn't know it at the time. Jack confirmed it.

"Before I knew it, I lunged at the birthday boy. My teeth clenched tight enough to crack my molars, fists swinging ferociously, bashing his jaw, my nails tearing at his eye sockets.

"'Get off me!' he yelled, but I didn't stop. I kicked. I clawed. I felt joy beating him in that champagne room, and if Harris hadn't burst in, I fear I would have killed him with my bare hands. Even scarier, I wouldn't have felt bad about it.

"'Mafia! I saw the signal but the floor is packed! Had to muscle my way through!' Harris pulled me off the customer.

"I slapped Harris across the face, tears streaming. 'He could have seriously hurt me! He's twice my size! He could have killed me!' I yelled, the birthday boy's blood dripping from my fingers.

"'I know. I'm sorry, Mafia.' Harris grabbed the customer by the neck, effortlessly lifting him from the floor with one hand.

"'I can't do this! I can't do this anymore! I hate this. Who am I? I don't know! I don't even know who I am? I'm leaving! Now kick his ass some more and throw him out into the street! Don't stop punching his face in until he's scared he might die!'

"'Gladly,' Harris promised, balling his fists.

"Back in the dressing room I got dressed, still heaving from the tussle.

"Valentine barged in. 'Well if it isn't the little golden girl. Bet you made a lot of money tonight. Bet you're not out here begging like the rest of us bottom feeders.' I ignored her at first. 'How much you make tonight? Tell me. How much? Bet it's more than I made. I used to make so much money, remember? I used to spread it out and lay on it back here and take selfies, you remember that. Fun times.'

"'Go away, Valentine. I'm not in the mood.'

"'It's early; you leaving?'

"'Yes! Now go away!'

"'Where you going?'

"'None of your business. Don't you have a worm in a tequila bottle to go chase?'

"'Is that blood on you?' she asked, dropping her beer, running to my aid.

"'Yes, it's fine. I'm fine. Just get back out there on the floor before you piss off Jack.'

"'Stop! Please!' she yelled. I'll admit, her tone startled me. 'Don't you know that I care? Don't you know that I still pray for you? Yes, I pray too, a devil like me. I've watched you grow. I watched you! I helped you to become so strong, and now when I'm weak you leave me! You leave!' She was crying. 'Don't you know that I love you still? I still fear for you. Need you.'

"Valentine reached for the nearest rag and soaked it in alcohol. She quietly cleaned my hands.

"The silence was awkward, and I didn't really know what to say so I just apologized. 'I should have never given up on you so easily. I should have been there for you.'

"'No, it's my fault for being so shady and unpredictable. What were you supposed to do, trust me again and let me put you in another bad situation?'

"'I'm sorry.'

"'Don't be. I'm nothing but junkie. I used to read all those pretty poems you'd write when you'd fall asleep. You'll go places. Me, I'll be dancing until the day I die. I wasn't built for anything else. I'm not even a good dancer anymore.'

"'Don't say that. You're the greatest entertainer that ever lived.' We hugged.

"'Look, I'd love to stay and talk this out some more, but I just can't right now. I gotta get out of here. I need to go find Halo. I need someone to keep an eye on Alice.'

"'I'll do it.'

"I hesitated. 'I … promised her I'd keep her safe.'

"'Please, let me. I'll make you proud. Let me show you that I wanna change.'

"'Okay. Don't let me down.'

"'I won't let you down ever again. We can be best friends again. It'll be Valentine and Mafia just like old times. I'm gonna fly right. I really am this time. I'll prove it to you. I'm gonna find Alice and won't let her out of my sight. That's a promise. I got your back, Mafia.'

"'Okay. Thank you.'

"'Do you believe in me?'

"'Yes, I do.'

"'That's all I need. I'm on my way up, Mafia, out of this dark place. I'm going to make you proud! You'll see!'"

Chapter 18

"It's a simple man's dream, to love his job. People gotta work. You gotta make money if you wanna eat. Ain't nobody gonna give you nothing in this world free of charge. So for me to say I find joy I my craft, it's a real blessing. Now I know what you're thinking. What man wouldn't wanna be surrounded by hard bodies every night for a living? But that's just a lucky perk, I swear. I like getting up here away from all the action on the floor. Being way up here in the booth, I see things. I become an all, knowing eye in the sky. I've seen things you wouldn't believe. I know these girls, they're like my daughters. I look after them as best I can. I watch them scampering down below like little fire ants, hustling. They've all been where you are right now, sitting up here with me, so uncertain.'

"Saddle looked over at Alice with genuine pity. 'You can sit here as long as you like, won't bother me none.'

"'Do you think she left me, maybe forgot about me?'

"'Anything's possible, but it's not like Mafia to leave without tipping out and taking herself out of rotation.'

"'She said to wait here for her if I needed her.'

"'I'll call for her on the mic, okay?' He spoke into the mic: 'Mafia, you're needed at the DJ booth. Mafia, DJ booth please.'

"'Hey, y'all calling for Mafia?' Valentine asked, climbing into the DJ booth.

"'Yeah, we called for Mafia. Not you. You seen her in the last hour?'

"'Actually, I did.'

"'You did?' Alice asked hopefully.

"'Yeah, unfortunately she had to go. It was personal. You must be the precious cargo she asked me to look after.'

"'Cargo?' Alice asked, twiddling her thumbs.

"'I'm Valentine. Don't think we've met. I'm never on time anymore. Mafia asked me to keep an eye on you for the night.'

"Saddle interrupted. 'I don't know. Jack said—'

"'To hell with what Jack said, Saddle. I know this business like the back of my hand. I've been stripping since I was old enough to buy a fake ID. How do you think Mafia got so savvy? Here, come with me,' Valentine said, holding out her hand.

"Saddle eyed Valentine. 'Wait now. If Jack told her to stick with Mafia, he did if for a reason. Maybe she should just stay here with me.'

"Valentine grew furious. 'I'm so sick and tired of everyone treating me like a walking disaster! I'm not a complete screw-up! Don't forget whose hard work helped keep this place alive when the club wasn't pulling in a dime. Why am I suddenly incapable of handling simple tasks, huh? Because I'm not riding around on a horse as high as yours?'

"Valentine stepped closer to Alice. 'Listen here little girl, there's money to be made on the floor. The quicker you make it, the sooner you can leave. You don't wanna be around when the later crowd rolls in. That's when the real weirdos come out to play. You ain't gonna make a penny sitting up here with rain man Saddle over here. What you gonna do? Make a big girl decision for once in your life.'

"Reluctantly, Alice grabbed hold of Valentine's hand and the two of them quickly disappeared in the crowd.

"Concerned, Saddle immediately phoned Mafia. 'Hey it's me, Saddle. I need you to call me back when you get this message. Your precious cargo has been hijacked by pirate Valentine.'"

Chapter 19

"It was freezing. I remember my bones shaking as I stood knocking at Princeton's door. My bare feet were nearly numb. I knocked for a while with no answer. For a moment it occurred to me that he wasn't home or just didn't want to see me. Maybe we were over. I almost walked away but then he opened the door. I must've looked so pathetic, standing there like a feeble ally cat.

"My eyes were optimistic, praying there was still a chance for us. 'Will you still have me?'

"Princeton noticed the blood on my face. 'Reese, what happened? You're bleeding. Where are your shoes?' he asked, tilting my head to assess the damage.

"'My heart stopped beating tonight, longer than a second. Maybe a minute or more. Not in the literal sense of course. What I mean is, something happened and after it happened I considered the fact that I very well could have lost my life. What if I left this world behind, with you still in it not knowing how much you really meant to me? It was at that moment I realized that you were right. I don't belong there. I belong next to you. Is the offer still good?' I tried my hardest to keep from crying.

"'Are you hurt? Who did this to you? I'll haul them to jail myself right now.' It was true. I was hurt. I was in pain, but my pending question hanging unanswered in the blistering chill was far more pertinent.

"'Is the offer still good?' I asked again.

"Princeton stepped closer, his palm warm against my aching face. 'Reese, real love does not expire nor does it depreciate. It only grows.' His embrace was unspeakably gentle, and in it I wept.

"I buried my face in Princeton's chest, and with a single deep inhale I fell to pieces for the first time in a long time. I felt his tears streaming down my neck. I never heard a single solitary sniffle but I felt his cry.

"'Am I safe again?' I asked.

"'You'll always be safe from now on.'

"'I'll do it. I'll quit. I won't dance anymore.' I went inside with Princeton. He tucked me in and watched over me all night."

Chapter 20

"'You ever did a lap dance before?' Valentine asked with a promiscuous stare.

"A nervous Alice answered honestly, 'No, never.'

"'What? Not even at home, for a boyfriend?'

"'I've never had a boyfriend,' Alice admitted, embarrassed.

"'That's just plain old sad. Suddenly everything about you makes sense. Well, there's a first time for everything. You see that group of construction workers over there in the corner,' Valentine said, pointing.

"'Yeah.'

"'I want you to go over there, flip your hair, and tell them you need a drink. Once you down it, tell them you're feeling frisky and you're dying to give a lap dance. Make them feel like giving them a dance is an honor. Men have big egos and they'll eat it up. Then drag 'em to the lap dance room. Even if they don't want one, they'll pay, so they don't look cheap or homosexual in front of the rest of the gang.'

"'Lap dance room? What's going to happen in there?'

"'It's called the lap dance room. Instructions don't get no plainer than that, sweetheart.'

"Alice did as she was told, and before long, she was in the back giving multiple dances to multiple customers infatuated with the club's fresh new face.

"Valentine sat at the bar, watching closely as promised.

"'Valentine? Is that you?' asked an approaching patron, adjusting his glasses.

"Valentine looked up, acknowledging the gentleman, an annoying old customer who'd grown quite fond of her company over the years. 'Yes, that's *my* name you're wearing out. Too bad I don't remember *yours*. Must not have made a good enough impression,' she replied, quickly turning her attention back to Alice.

"'Still a charmer I see. So …'

"'So … what?' Valentine asked, annoyed.

"'Long time no see. How have you been?'

"'I'm just grand. Can't you tell?' she snapped.

"'Glad to hear it. How about I buy you a drink? You still drinking that strong local moonshine Jack keeps stashed?'

"'No thanks.'

"'Come on now. One won't kill you. Bought some of my friends here with me this go around. They're looking to have a good time. If you got the time, we got the money. What do you say? Wanna get out of here with us?'

"'No.'

"'No?' he repeated, as if he'd heard wrong.

"'That's what I said.'

"'Did I mention we got some free party favors? The kind you like, guaranteed to get you lifted.'

"Valentine hesitated, thinking of the high she chased night after night but resisted, thinking of her promise to Mafia. 'No thanks. I'm not boarding that flight tonight,' she answered firmly.

"'What, are you checking into rehab or something? Gotta meet with your parole officer in the morning for a piss test?'

"'No, neither. I just gotta do something for my friend. Don't wanna let her down again. I need my wits about me. Now please, go away.'

"It seemed as if *no* was her final answer. 'Well, fine. Maybe some other time.'

"'Yeah, maybe,' she muttered, stretching her neck for a better view of Alice, who was doing just fine, making money and following the club rules.

"Pride slightly wounded, the wayward partier walked away to join his crew, but on his way back to the table, he stopped the nearest waitress. 'Hey there, darling. How would you like to make a hundred dollars in five minutes?'

"Her inexperience was made obvious by the look of incontrollable excitement that rose on her face at the sound of what every dancer in the club would've considered chump change. 'A hundred dollars? That's more than I've made all night!'

"'Is that right? Well, this whole hundred can be yours. All you gotta do is bring a drink to that woman sitting alone at the bar. Say it's from an anonymous customer.'

"'Sure, I can do that!'

"'And before you give it to her, sprinkle a little bit of this in it, give it stir,' the partier said, sliding a small bag into the waitress's hand with the folded hundred dollar bill.

"'I don't know … I could get into trouble.'

"'Trouble? Heck no, I know the owners,' he lied. 'I do it all the time. She's just a nice girl who needs to have a nice, relaxed night. I'm sure you've heard of her reputation. Trust me, she's nicer when she gets a little helper like this. You'd be doing her a huge favor. I'll bet she thanks you for it later.'

"'Are you sure I won't get into trouble?'

"'Trust me, she won't mind. Everybody likes a pick-me-up. But this is our little secret, okay?'

"The waitress walked away with the drink. 'Hey, you're Valentine, right?'

"'Who wants to know? Surely not you. What business could a crappy cocktail waitress have with me?' Valentine snapped.

"'It's this drink, somebody bought it for you.'

"'Percy must really wanna be featured on the next segment of to catch a predator.'

"'It's not from him. A secret admirer sent it over.'

"'Secret admirer?'

"'Yeah, too shy to come over so he sent me instead. He said you're just to pretty to approach.'

"Valentine looked down at the drink and then back at Alice, who was still doing fine. 'Who made this drink?'

"'I did.'

"'Waitresses don't make drinks, bartenders we've been working with for years that we trust make the drinks around here. Sage makes my drinks, only her. Jack should fire you.'

"'But I watched her earlier! I was really careful and I mixed it right! Please don't go tell on me! I really need this job!'

"'Has it been out of your sight, even for a minute?'

"'No, of course not.'

"'Okay.' Valentine accepted it. 'Get from behind the bar and be sure to thank this mysterious Mr. Nice Guy for me.'

"Thirty-four minutes later, Valentine held her left hand out in front of her face, waving it quickly from left to right as if to test the accuracy of her vision. Something was wrong. The colors trailing behind her fingertips were psychedelic and familiar. Her diaphragm felt warm and her toes were tingly. 'Impossible,' Valentine muttered, calculating the number of drinks she'd consumed. *Drunk? Already?* she thought. *That can't be right. Buzzed maybe ...*

"As the hours went by, Valentine's inebriation worsened. Her attempts to offer companionship to customers were turned down, which only made her drink more. And more.

"Alice approached the bar. 'Valentine! Val, Look! I can't believe it. I made over five hundred dollars! I've never seen so much money all at once. I was doubtful at first, but I think I can do it. I'm going to save the house and the business, you wait and see. He'll be so proud, my daddy! Val! Did you hear me?'

"'Yeah, I heard you!' Valentine grunted, annoyed. 'You made half a grand. Good for you. You think that's something to celebrate? Bet you got a long way to go, a lot more money to make to get you where you need to be.'

"Alice sat beside Valentine, discouraged. 'Yeah, I guess you're right. But this is only my first night. If I work just as hard every night, I'll make the money in no time. Just like Mafia said I would.'

"'I know a way you can make it all tonight,' Valentine said.

"'Really? How?'

"'You wanna go to a party? All you have to do is look pretty. Look pretty and serve.'"

Chapter 21

"When I woke the next morning, I had missed vague texts and calls from Saddle. Valentine had called twenty-two times and left more than a dozen voice mails. I deleted them without listening, assuming they were excuses as to why she'd failed me again.

"'How long have I been asleep?' I asked, rubbing the crust from my heavy eyes.

"'Not too long. Mostly you just tossed and turned. You eventually settled down right when the sun came up,' he answered, yawning. 'You're a creature of habit.'

"'Did you get any sleep at all?'

"'Not a single wink. I wanted to keep a close watch on you, considering that lump on your forehead and all.'

"'Now I feel bad.'

"'Don't. I enjoyed watching you sleep. You were peaceful; at ease for once,' he replied sitting down beside me in bed. 'Reese, I was wondering. Did you mean everything you said last night, about quitting?'

"'Yeah. I've never felt more sure about anything in my entire life.'

"Relief settled on his face. 'I'm so glad to hear you say that. Do you need me to come down there with you, help you clean out your locker? Pack up all your things? I won't put my uniform on and embarrass you.'

"'No, I can do it. Go to work. Cover your shift. I'll be fine. I'll go in early, before everyone gets there, avoid all the awkward goodbyes. I don't want anyone trying to convince me to stay. My mind is made up and that's that.'

"'I want you to call me the minute you get to the club, and I want you to call me the second you leave. Then I want you to call me again once you're back here safe, with the doors locked and the alarm set. It'll be that way until I find the man who did this to you. I need to know you're okay. I'll worry. I want you in this bed, cozy, waiting for me when I get home. We have a future to plan.'

"'I'll check in, I triple promise.'"

Chapter 22

"The air inside was thick inside Club Malice, difficult to inhale in an emotionally tense manner. An uncomfortable silence caused me to catch my breath instead of the usual cigarette smog.

"Jack sat at the bar with a drink in hand. There was an unsettled look on his face. In fact his entire disposition appeared heavy. Saddle sat at the bar a few stools down right next to Harris. It was the first time I'd ever seen Percy the pervert without a shot glass. They all seemed oddly sullen, and Sage never looked up at all.

"I walked over, leaned on the bar. 'Hey, what's going on?' I asked.

"No one looked up. 'Jack? Saddle? What is it?'

"There was no answer right away. They all simply exchanged glances, eyeing one another as if to nominate a barer of bad news.

"Jack emptied his glass with a single swallow. He then turned to me, eyes tinted red. They were damp in the corners. I'd never seen Jack mirror an ounce of emotion, not once. So I knew whatever it was, it was bad. 'I'm sorry, Mafia.'

"'Sorry for what? That jerk birthday boy from last night? It's okay. That wasn't your fault. That lightweight hit like a girl toddler. Next time we should serve his drinks out of a sippy cup. It happens. I'm not made of glass. Nothing a little antibiotic ointment and aspirin won't fix,' I said, eyeing Harris's peculiar sympathetic expression.

"'No. Not that.'

"'Okay, then for what?'

"'The girls, they're all here. Let Sage walk you on back to the dressing room. You all should be together right now.'

"Sage came from behind the bar. She grabbed my arms and pulled me in close. She didn't say a word as she ushered my body through the tables, maneuvering the chairs so that I could make my way through. We entered the dressing room and I saw our fellow dancers, our friends, standing lined up like toy soldiers along the vanity mirrors. They were all crying, comforting one another. Consoling one another. At my entering, they all stopped and stared.

"'What are you guys doing here so early? Customers won't be here for at least two more hours. What's going on?'

"Whisper approached, her face pink and her voice soft, words slow. 'It's Valentine.'

"'What did she do now?' I asked, rolling my eyes.

"'She didn't show up at her sitter's to pick up the kids. The sitter started calling around. Couldn't find her anywhere.'

"'Okay, well, did they try the motel off the freeway or the basketball court? Sometimes she goes to the park, sits on the swings and loses track of the time. I'll try her cell.'

"Whisper grabbed my wrist and squeezed real tight. 'No, don't call, sweetie. That's not necessary. They already found her.'

"'Okay, so problem solved.'

"'No. They found her, but it's not good.'

"My eyes scanned the room from left to right and squinted as I tried to comprehend why Halo was trembling. 'I don't understand,' I said as Olive began to sob even harder and Sage took Olive in her arms.

"'Before dawn, a homeless man rummaging around the park stumbled upon what he thought was a woman in distress. Cops showed up, found a woman who'd been severely beaten. Unfortunately, she wasn't breathing. They didn't even call an ambulance, there was no need. Wasn't any life left. Official identification is pending on account of family being scattered and uncooperative, but police showed up here questioning Jack after they found a Club Malice card with her driver's license. They're certain it's Valentine.'

"'What did you just say, Whisper?'

"'Valentine's dead.'

"I felt weak. I'd heard clearly what Whisper had said, but it hadn't registered right away. 'No, it can't be. There must be some sort of mistake. When I left here last night, she was sober. She was better.'

"'Valentine's tattoos—they sat Jack down and showed him pictures, compared them to her hire file. The license was the same and the cops had already matched her face to a past arrest record. There's no mistake. It's her.'

"'She called. She tried to call me, but I ...' My knees gave out. Whisper helped me settle my weight on the floor.

"I wept. All of us wept. We sat on the floor in one big hug, stretching our arms across one another's back forming a circle. Our mourning was a mutual aching and in that moment I saw it, our individual struggles. I saw a fear we all shared, that the lifestyle would swallow us before we had a chance to get out. We were all equal. No one better or worse than the other. No one was safe. We were all just women, looking for a way to make it in a very scary world. And we'd just lost one of our own. She was ours. And she was gone now.

"Once I could stand again, I peeled my name tag off my locker and stuffed my duffle. 'I'm leaving. I'm not just taking a few nights off like I did every other time I stormed out. I'm going for good. I brought God with me when I came to this place and I'm taking him with me now so I'm not sure where life is going to take me but I know I'll be all right. Is anyone coming with me?'

"No one answered. I wiped my tears away and turned to Whisper. 'If we all love each other as much as we claim, we'll find a way to stay in one another's lives. Take care of them.' That was the last thing I said to her.

"'I'll never stop. We'll see you on the outside,' Whisper promised. 'I expect to see you at the ribbon cutting when I open my pole studio. I'm gonna need some good instructors. I can't think of anybody better than the Mafia princess. I'm gonna put a big picture of us all on the wall inside. You wait and see, the world is gonna be proud of who we turned out to be,' she said as I walked out of the dressing room for the last time.

"That was the last thing Whisper said to me. And I had smiled at her and said, 'I wouldn't miss it for the world.'"

Chapter 23

"I never told Jack I was leaving. When I walked up to the bar again, he looked down at my bag and knew without me saying so. We just hugged. Goodbyes made Harris feel funny, so his idea of a hug was quick athletic shoulder pat, as if to get it over with. Saddle respectfully shook my hand as if we'd served in war together.

"I made my way to the exit and walked out without looking back. Once outside I stood for a second thinking about Valentine, reminiscing. When I closed my eyes, I could almost hear her laugh. I thought about my first night on stage. I thought of my first cry. I thought of all the dressing room lip-syncing contests, us singing into curling irons while taking silly group selfies to pass the time. It was odd, the sense of relief I felt, and I wasn't afraid anymore, to close that door. In fact, I felt like it was long overdue. I'd collected my confidence but overstayed my welcome. I took a deep breath, and I smiled big. It was then that I saw the silhouette of the stranger approaching.

"The shadow emerged eerily from the darkness of the parking lot. The bulbs on the neon sign danced, and with each flickering blink the shadowy figure became more defined. It grew closer and closer. The loose gravel crushing beneath the assailant's feet sent shivers through my body but I couldn't move.

"'Alice? Is that you?' I asked, slightly frightened. The darkness's ability to compromise the certainty of the rogue's identity scared me in a weird way. I was still unsure at this point so I called her name again, hoping for an answer the second time.

I waited, but there was no longer any question. I could clearly see her face. It was Alice. 'Mafia? What are you doing here? You're early. You're not supposed to be here yet.'

"'I know. I only came to gather my things, and then I heard the awful news.'

"'Awful news?'

"'Yeah. It's Valentine.'

"'The body everyone's talking about around town? It was Valentine?' she asked, pulling the hood of her coat from the top of her hair.

"'Yeah,' I answered, sobbing uncontrollably again. 'I can barely say it out loud. I just can't believe it. She's really gone.'

"'*That's* awful news? Dead Valentine? Sounds more like karma than bad news,' she muttered, eyes wide and empty.

"I clutched my crucifix necklace tight, shocked by the sound of such heartlessness. 'I know you didn't really know her or care for her. But that's a horrible thing to say, Alice, a horribly godless insult to us who cared for her.'

"'A horrible thing to say?' Alice laughed. 'No it's not. In fact, I'm far too kind. But then again, I'm a lady. There are many worse things I could say about Valentine. I'll keep them to myself. Wouldn't wanna hurt your feelings.'

"'Have you no heart? Speaking ill of the dead! She didn't deserve to die like that. No one does.'

"Alice stepped closer, and I could see the denseness of her pupils outlined in red. 'Who are you to say who suffers and who doesn't? The death should suit the amount of havoc and disloyalty and unkindness a person stained upon others during their time here on earth. At least Valentine was rewarded release, sweet death. She'll never dream of this hell ever again or relive the bad things others have done to her. It can't haunt her. So you see? Silver lining.'

"Alice shoved past me and headed for the club entrance.

"'Alice, wait,' I said, pulling at her sleeve. 'It's obvious something's wrong. I'm so sorry for leaving you and for whatever happened to you. I know I can't fix it, but maybe you and I could just sit and talk for a minute. There's a diner over on the upper east side. The fry cook knows we work late hours, so he makes us breakfast long before opening, the best waffles in the whole city. Any topping you want, my treat.'

"'*Now* you want to take care of me?" she asked sardonically. 'No thank you,' she mumbled, staring down at discarded cigarette butts on the cracked concrete. 'I can't. I got something I gotta do right now.'

"'Please, Alice. I want to help you. I want to be there for you.'

"'I said no! In fact, I want you to get out of my face! Leave, Mafia! You need to get the hell out of here! Before I change my mind. You— there's still hope for you. This is not your fault. Jack said good things about you. "Quicker than a ghost in the dark and sharper than any manmade blade but just as trustworthy. She's got a good heart." He was right. You were the light in all this, and for that reason you can't be here tonight. It's everyone's final set. It's last call, so clear out.'

"'Last call? I don't understand.'

"'There's nothing to understand because this doesn't concern you, Mafia! Leave! Now!' Alice had begun to yell at me, but her eyes held a peculiar sacrificial beckoning. The sound of the bugs frying in the neon sign was the only thing I could hear besides my own frantic heartbeat and her heavy, demonic heaving.

"'You don't belong here, Mafia, and neither did I. What business do angels have in hell?'

"Alice opened the door and I watched her disappear into the blue light shining from the slot machines. The door slammed. I turned to walk away, dialing Princeton, but before he could answer I heard the sound of the big steel lock entombing Alice inside with everyone. I stopped dead in my tracks, dropping my phone and duffle. I knew then what was about to happen.

"My breath was hot, showing white against the night air, puffing small clouds as my breathing quickened. What was coming next would be bad. I could feel it all over my body.

"The screaming began. I dashed for the door and pulled hard but it wouldn't budge. The first shot rang. The screams got louder.

"'Alice No! No!' I yelled, beating the steel with my fist, and I remember how it felt, like a block of ice freezing out my plea. I heard more gunshots and I kept on pounding. 'Alice, no! Please!'

"I heard Jack's voice: 'Everybody get down!'

"Shots continued. It could have been ten more, it could have been a hundred. I can't recall, but I do recall falling to my knees, clawing the door so hard that my acrylic nails separated from the skin.

"Banshee cries—that's what it sounded like, their perishing. As they wailed, I wept. Even though I wasn't inside I knew they were all dying.

"Suddenly the shots stopped. I pressed my cheek to the door, listening. All was momentarily still. 'Alice,' I whispered, lightly tapping with my knuckles. 'Please let me inside,' I begged, praying she'd unbolt the lock and I could convince her to let me in and help the victims.

"Alice never answered. I could hear her though, shuffling around inside. I listened to her shatter bottles of liquor from behind the bar. Then I started to smell smoke, and fumes began to seep under the door. She'd flooded the club floor with highly flammable alcohol and set it ablaze while still inside. Poor Alice wanted to die too.

"I panicked, trying to kick and punch my way in. 'Alice, you gotta get outta there!'

"Then there was the big boom, an explosion that erupted with great force. It sent me flying. I landed several feet away, and the noise was suddenly far away, like a thousand leagues under the sea. I was dizzy, and the floating flame debris looked like snowflakes and fireflies raining down on me as I lay on my back looking up at the sparks.

"There was one last scream, but it quickly ceased with a bullet and I was happy. Why? Because there was no more suffering. I was happy because I didn't have to sit there and listen to them burn to death.

"Sirens soon followed. The next thing I remember was my Princeton. He scooped me up and tossed me over his shoulder. Before the ambulance doors shut, I took one last look. The club was completely engulfed, burning to the ground, and I knew they'd never reach back, but I reached for them as if to say, 'Come with me.' But it was too late."

Chapter 24

"There was light all around us when I was dreaming. The light weaved majestically in and out of our bodies as we stood with our arms linked at the elbow. I envisioned us in the same dressing room we'd prepared our bodies in a million times, but it appeared cleaner than ever before and I couldn't see our feet. It was as if we were all floating. Our heads were bowed, eyes closed. I led the prayer, just like always.

"'Lord, as I look around this room I see many things that don't make you proud. We have things inside ourselves that you didn't put there; no, these things were planted here by the world. But your love is for everyone and so is the right to pray. The Bible says where two or three gather in your name, you'd be there in the midst. So here we are in solidarity, all together seeking your protection once again. We ask to please pardon our profane footsteps as we tread heavily across the coal. We meditate on your love. We lean on it. This path we've chosen is not well lit. So we gather as much strength as we can, knowing that because we truly belong to you we can never be owned by anything or anyone because we are not slaves. We can never be bought because we were created in such a precious way that our worth can never be numbered. We will not be afraid tonight even though the ones waiting for us outside this dressing room serve a devil that works overtime. Why not? Because we believe in a God who never sleeps and does not count sheep. Send a few more angels to watch over us until morning comes again. But until then, forgive us from being misplaced, separated from our destiny temporarily. Stay with us, and please don't let us sin so severely that we forfeit our purpose. Amen.'

"When the prayer so over, they all looked up at me with smiles more beautiful that anything I'd ever seen on this side of heaven. They didn't speak, just slowly dispersed. And when they were gone, I knew what they wanted me to do.

"I could feel Princeton's hand clasping mine. His grip was strong, and he squeezed even tighter as he noticed my eyes opening. My vision was blurry at first, but when the fuzziness faded, his face was plain to see. 'Reese, you're awake! Thank God. I was so worried.'

"'What's happening?' I asked, trying to get out of bed.

"'No, stay still. You need to stay in bed. You've got a broken bone and some serious contusions,' he said, reaching for a cup of room temperature water to moisten my throat. I sipped the straw as he dabbed my head with a damp towel. 'What do you remember?'

"I paused and tried to recollect as best I could. 'I remember, boom.'

"'Boom?'

"'Yeah. There was Alice. I saw Alice at the club. I talked to her about Valentine. Valentine …'

"'Dead …'

"'Yeah.'

"'Then what?'

"'Then …' I stopped talking and tears began to well. 'She …'

"Princeton climbed in the hospital bed next to me and pulled me close.

"'Are they really all gone?'

"'Yeah. Everyone. They released the names and photos this morning. They linked Valentine's murder to the club, saying as how the club was the last place she was seen alive and everyone else was murdered less than twenty-four hours later.'

"'This can't be happening.'

"'I'm sorry. It's happening. And I have a feeling the worst is yet to come for you.'

"'What do you mean?'

"'You're the only person who survived. They're calling it a massacre. It's all over the news, Reese. And you're the only person who knows what happened. They're calling you the sole survivor of the biggest mass murder in the town's history. I'm sorry for the hell your about to go through. Your life is never going to be the same.'

Chapters 25

"'Get back! Move it! Have some decency, folks,' Princeton demanded, shoving back the press. 'Make way! Touch her and you'll have a harassment suit on your hands to deal with!'

"Many cameras flashed from all sides. Almost every bystander recorded my hospital discharge for instant social media upload. It was difficult to maneuver through the hoard with my leg in pieces, but finally we made it to the car and they still wouldn't let up. I felt the car rocking from the pressure on both sides, people leaning over the hood, trying to get closer for a better look at my injuries, maybe capture some of my sadness.

"'Let's get you home so you can rest,' Princeton said, honking his horn to clear a path.

"'I don't wanna go home.'

"'Okay. Where do you wanna go? Just tell me and we'll go.'

"'Take me to see them.'

"'Them? You mean …'

"'Yes. Take me to their graves.'

"Princeton hesitated. 'I really don't think it's a good idea. You're still too weak, Reese. Let it all soak in a while longer. Then we can get some flowers for them and visit the proper way, when you're in a more stable mind set.'

"'They're dead, Princeton. I don't think they really care if we bring flowers.'

"'It's so soon. Are you sure you wanna do this?'

"'You asked me where I wanted to go. I'm telling you where I wanna be. Are you going to take me or not? My leg might be busted but I can walk there if I have to. Please don't underestimate my pride.'

"It was as if there'd never been a building there before. Everything was gone. The club had been leveled to a mound of fresh soil and burnt wood chips.

"Princeton attempted to help me out of the passenger seat, pulling at my seat belt. 'I can do it!' I barked, eyes locked on the shadowy ground nearest the tracks. 'Would you please get my crutches for me?'

"'Do you want me to come with you in case you get tired?'

"'No. I wanna go alone, if that's all right.'

"I stood before them, the stones, graves neatly aligned deep in the scorched land. First there was Jack, of all trades. His tombstone read *Master of many things, good and bad.* To his right lay Whisper with the beautiful hair, whose real name was Hailey. Next was January—Joan—who never wanted anything but a healthy baby of her own. I'll be honest, I cried a bit more when I moved on to Halo's grave. Everything she ever did was for her daughter. Taunie was the name her mother had given her, the one who kissed her daughter's picture each night before we hit the floor. *Disgusting adulterer, go to hell and rot there* was spray painted on Percy's stone. Obviously his wife had been there to visit. Guess she wasn't happy with the whole town knowing her pervert of a husband died in a topless bar, but who could blame her? Sage's grave made me feel a sense of peace concerning the decision my heart had recently made.

"I kissed her stone and looked back at Princeton. 'I know what you said, but he's different. Give him a chance. I think I might love him. Is that okay with you, Jeanie?' Jeanie, that was her name. Never did hear the story as to how she came to be called Sage. Maybe she was who she was long before she ever came to Club Malice.

"All the way down past Saddle's grave, the man who helped pass the time by sharing wise parables, I found Valentine's spot. Her stone had no name, only the letter F and the number 14, per my request. F for February and the number 14 to mark her day, Valentine's day. And since I refused to call her Valentine from that point on, I spoke her name out loud for the first and last time. 'I'm gonna miss you something fierce. Goodbye, Tierney. Rest as peacefully as you can. Who needs the shore when you can have the sky?'

"Some arrests were made, some misdemeanor charges filed on everyone who attended that party, the last place Valentine was seen alive with Alice. Scoundrels have a way of sticking together, especially when there's murder accusations. Maybe Valentine tried to steal from them, they caught her, and got mad. Maybe Valentine left the party way too loaded, underestimated how much she could handle, and died at the hands of some maniac who had nothing to do with this story. Maybe she got sick or passed out and they panicked, tried to cover it up by beating her to the point that she was barely recognizable, dumped her hoping no one would care enough to go looking for her.

"There were rumors that Valentine had drugged Alice in an attempt to get her to comply with the sick party demands. After hours of unresponsive raping, Valentine feared she'd administered a lethal dosage by accident. She panicked and begged them all to help dump Alice. When the partiers refused, Valentine tried to get rid of Alice herself. They say Alice woke from her trance before Valentine could fatally wound her. Some say Alice then attacked Valentine in a coma-like rage, crying out for her innocence back, and when Valentine said there was no return value, Alice snapped. Then she broke into her dad's pawn shop and stole the guns with enough ammunition to kill everyone in the club.

"Princeton says that everything happens for a reason. If Valentine hadn't died, the girls wouldn't have shown up until way later to suit up. More customers could have arrived in that time. There could have been way more victims. Who's to say? The questions and answers may never level one another out evenly. We might not ever know what really happened. This small town will turn it into a local folk tale to be retold over and over, to strike fear in little children for years to come, especially around Halloween. I have that nightmare now too, that one year in October I'll get a knock on the door and some kid who knows nothing about this horror will be dressed up as one of my friends, thinking it's some cool costume. What's scarier though, seeing a fake costume covered in fake blood or having one of those future trick or treaters lift up their mask, reminding me that a cheap plastic mask is as close as I'll ever be to seeing them again?"

Chapter 25

"You hope for the best, Diana. *Wise beyond my years.* I hate when people say that because I wish some of the wisdom I banked didn't have to be obtained by surviving so much misery. But I am wise. I don't want you to misinterpret that as a self-proclaimed character trait. You can't help what you see, no more than you can help the lesson's you're forced to learn in life. Some nights I'd lay awake thinking about all the bad things I did in life. I thought about the day I torched my beloved's car. When I was seven years old, I was told I was I couldn't have any cookies. I waited until my mother was fast asleep and talked my older sister into getting the cookies for me. You see, I was too short, but she was just all enough for the grab. We tiptoed into the kitchen, retrieved the jar, and stuffed our faces until the cookies were all gone.

"I woke up the next morning to the sound of my mother scolding my sister. My sister never said a word about it being my idea, and she never ratted me out. When she was killed, I went to my mother and finally came clean about that night we stole dessert.

"She smiled and said to me, 'I figured she *didn't act alone.* But when I asked her about it she simply replied, "Momma, I'm older. I should have known better.""

"I thought about the time I was eleven. Skylar Finley, the prettiest rich brat in school, sabotaged my dress right before the Miss Mossvilla pageant. We didn't have much money, so imagine how crushed I was when she purposely spilled grape juice on my white handmade dress right before the talent round. I ended up winning second place to her, and when it was time for the group photograph, I shoved her from behind, causing her to fall flat on her smug face. Her front two teeth never grew back properly, and she never really smiled after that.

"I also thought about all the things I'd seen at Club Malice. Yeah, I lost a lot of sleep calculating it all up, the bad. The only way I'd ever get to sleep was contemplating God's love for all of us, so thankful that he never asked us for perfection. I mean, I know he's not proud of the times we fall short but I know he doesn't see a monster when he sees me. God would never call me by any of the names cruel people called me. Every night before bed, I just asked God. Please, let my good outweigh my bad. And when I finally see the gates once my life is spent, I'll hope for the best.

"What about you, Diana?"

"What about me, Reese?"

"Do you calculate your deeds? The good ones? Bad ones? Do you ever regret the path you took? The destination was the same, so was your purpose. I'm sure you're right where you're supposed to be right now at this very moment in your life."

"I'm not quite sure where you're going with this," Diana said, squirming.

"I think you do," Reese said, uncrossing her legs, leaning forward. "When we first started, you asked me why I chose this station. You asked why I chose you. You see, the admiration of someone can push a person to achieve goals they never thought possible. It takes a real humble, hardworking person to take nothing and turn it into life that you can be proud of. A dream fulfilled. I once accepted what people had to say about me. Words really do hurt. By many, I've been persecuted the minute my profession was revealed, whether I honestly confessed it from my own mouth or suffered it being discovered through the investigation of miserable slackers who'd rather put me down than fix the things that make them so unhappy about themselves. I think about those dark times. Depression will kill you slowly. I could have easily accepted that defamation and spoke failure into my own life but no. That's where divine intervention steps in yet again. You."

"Me?" Diana asked, beginning to cry.

"Yes. You. If there was ever any question that people like me exist, outcasts who wander away for a while but come back and prove that there's no such thing as a lost cause. People like me, that walk through the shadows of death, fearing no evil. People like me, who can always swim back. People like you and me. Folks talk. I know who you are. I also know it's no reflection on who you are now. You see, you and I have more in common than people think. And if they can still respect you, if they still found a place for you, then how could they discard us? Who the hell are they to judge us, what cross did they die on?"

Diana swallowed the dry lump in her throat and forced a casual cough to mask the fact that tears were clearly visible to everyone in the interview room.

"No one cared about the things before, not even after this happened. Just the brutality. But the real horror is the soul sacrificing way we ventured inside the belly of the beast, that's where the real blood is, shed while being pulled in and out of right and wrong. And so we're clear, that brings the death total to thirteen, not eleven. Olive, Whisper, Sage, January, Halo, Harris, Jack, Percy the pervert, Alice, Valentine, Saddle, and two more."

"And what are their names?"

"Me, Mafia, and you, Diamond the doll face. You and I are alive only because those two gave their existence for us to be who we are. They served a purpose. I am also her, and she is also you. Now we're blessed with better versions of ourselves. We should be honoring them, not forgetting them or disgracing them by pretending they never existed. We're only us because of them. I know it may sound trippy, but I have a good feeling you understand exactly what I mean. You could have asked me the questions you wrote down. Hell, I wouldn't have answered them anyway, just a shrug is all you would've gotten. Rule number three is don't roll over on your club family. Use silence to protect their honor, alive or dead. I didn't write their story, so what gives me the right to expose every wrong turn? That's between them and God. I was taught by the best there ever was to never mind who she became before she died. I have more respect for her than people who thought they were better than her. I'm willing to bet you operate under that same ethic. Maybe you learned these things the same way I did."

The camera crew gasped and hid mumbles underneath their hands.

"I'd like to thank you from the bottom of my heart for having me here today. At least now viewers know they were people. At least now they know that there is more pain and strive in a brave spirt that has suffered than there will ever be in a person who has never ever had to overcome anything at all. We'll take that pain if it's the only way God can get us to kneel. What would have killed the average woman, we conquered. So maybe people should exercise a little respect and compassion when they handle folks, treat them more like Jesus would treat them and less like the devil. That's your beginning and end, Diana. Are there any more questions, Diana?"

Diana, clearing her throat again, looked around at all the staff members in the green room, including Kirk her admirer and Tommy. She looked down at her notes, all the inquisitive invasive questions that had been formulated before the interview commenced. For a moment, Diana considered asking them. "No. I think we're done."

"Cue camera one," Diana whispered, prompting Kirk to zoom in on her profile. "This has been a special in-depth look into the Club Malice massacre. I am Diana Foxx, and I thank you for tuning in."

Chapter 26

Diana slammed the trailer door behind her, ripping her lapel mic from her shirt, throwing it hard to the floor. Her breathing was rapid, almost as if she were experiencing an asthma attack. She collapsed in the middle of the floor, looking at each wall, a minute or two for each, just long enough to count all of her awards. There were plaques and trophies by the dozen. Diana thought back on all of her achievements, reminiscing the tiring dedication she'd spent trying to achieve her dreams. Eventually, she stood and grabbed an empty photo paper box. She began to pack her things.

"What are you doing?" Pete asked as he calmly stepped in.

"What does it look like? I'm leaving."

"Leaving? Why you wanna go and do that?"

"Well, I refused to do your bidding. You wanted me to destroy her and I didn't. I couldn't. We both know why."

"I didn't come in here to fire you, Diana."

Diana stopped packing and stared at Pete, shocked. "You didn't?"

"No. In fact I came to commend you."

"For what?"

"I've always respected your drive. You have talent. I see the way you own this place. People quiver in fear. My professor once lectured on the right and wrong way to head an empire. Is it better to be feared or loved? I weighed both options but could never give him a good enough answer. After months I still had nothing. He then said to me there wasn't a right answer. People who are feared will never know love. They will only have order. People who are loved will not always be afforded their proper civility for their loyalty. Because love is far too forgiving therefore it will be tried again and again. Your strut around here, it led me to believe you had forgotten where you'd come from. Being in the presence of an ingrate was my father's pet peeve. He was a man of great integrity. I took a different approach, obviously. I couldn't understand how he could be content just telling people whether to grab a raincoat. Why not reach higher? The look on your face tonight says you've felt every single pain she feels, don't you?"

Diana said nothing and held her chin up.

"What kind of man or woman would deny his or her own sin to avoid a little bit of shame? A shark like me? Maybe. But not you. You recorded restorative news this evening, not malicious exposure. And you did not cower, not even to me. That's the mark of a leader, challenging authority. If I can leave you with anything, I leave you with this: never let people think you're more than you are. Let them know who you were and weigh it against the person they see before them, then you will know true reverence. The promotion is yours," he said, turning to leave.

"Mr. Pete, wait!" Diana said, coming from around her desk to confront him face-to-face. "Before you do, there's something I'd like to say." Diana took a deep breath and folded her arms. "I paid my tuition one sweaty dollar tip at a time. I used to be a stripper, way back. I needed to say that out loud."

Pete smiled at her. "You done?"

"Yes."

"Okay. The promotion is still yours."

One year later ...

"This is Diana Foxx reporting live from our town's newest attraction, a new twist on hot fitness owned and operated by Reese Tania, Cambridge. Feeling unattractive, want to lose a few pounds? Come on down and book a few lessons with a real pole master. That's right, folks, its finally open for business. Reese Tania- Cambridge's Whisper Wings Pole Fitness Studio."

Reese stood near the back of the studio, finally away from the crowd, looking up at the mural Princeton had painted for her in secret.

It depicted seven women all bound by their hair looking up at the sky. It had been a surprise to find at the grand opening.

"I hope you don't mind my breaking in here and hanging it. I thought it would be nice to have them here with you today so they can see how well you've done," Princeton said, holding her hand.

"It's so beautiful," Reese said, tearing up.

"No, don't do that. No more tears. This is a celebration. I want to see you smiling."

"You make it easy to smile."

"Thank you, Mrs. Cambridge," Princeton answered, kissing her face.

"At this time I'd like you all to stand and raise your glasses as we welcome Reese up to say a few words," Diana announced.

Reese stood. "Thank you all for coming out today. I had a good friend once. She dreamed of opening a place like this. Sadly, she didn't live long enough to see her dream become a reality. I believe she's still here is spirit. So to make sure she's not forgotten, I opened this business in her memory. None of this would be possible without her, without people like us. I've hired performers who travel the world competing, mastering this art. They are going to teach you how to both downsize and mesmerize."

"Hey, I heard they call you Mafia, as in *the* Mafia, from Club Malice. Is that true? Are you the one who didn't die?" an opening attendee asked from the back of the mob.

Diana aggressively stepped forward. "She doesn't answer to that name anymore …"

"No, Diana, it's okay," Reese corrected. "Yeah, I'm her. She's me. We're one."

"I heard you used to be a wicked performer, extremely skilled on the pole," said the attendee, prompting sly smirks from the rest of the party. "Is that true?"

"I was alright," Reese answered.

"She's being modest," Princeton said, biting his lower lip at Reese.

"Well, show us a little something! Break in one of these poles! Make us wanna book a lesson in this studio!"

The crowd began to clap and agree.

"My dancing days are over."

"Oh, I see. You can't cut it anymore. You ain't 'bout that life," another member of the crowd snapped.

"What did you just say to me?" Reese asked, her face dangerously territorial, the way it used to be whenever she felt her reputation had been challenged during her nights at Club Malice.

"We're asking you for a show … if you still got it. If you can still keep up, prove it. Or are you scared?"

Reese looked over at her husband and then over at Diana, both of them grinning. "Diana?"

"Yes, Mafia," she answered.

"Put my song on. You all better have some dollars on you 'cause I don't work for free. Trust me. You gonna wanna tip this."

Printed in the United States
By Bookmasters